REXXOR

Grekk! The last thing his men needed were strange Terran women on our peaceful planet. But because of that grekking disease that wiped out most of our female population, here we are. The men were desperate for a female to do The Bonding with, and I was not going to let them down. I had to admit, it would be nice to have a mate to share my kingdom with. Giving my head a sharp shake, I scowled. NO! Kings did not need a woman. He couldn't afford to take care of a random woman on top of the duties to his planet. My tail twitched in agitation, this call to the Terran's government was going to suck.

I glanced at the hologram communication device in frustration. No matter how many times I used it, it was always a pain to figure out. Earth's Government had gifted me this weird technology during our first visit to their planet and it always annoyed me. I hailed the government after much hassle. Waiting, I drummed my claws on my throne impatiently. Finally, a withered face with a balding head and tufts of grey hair appeared suspended on the hologram. Damn Terrans were ugly I thought sourly as the man began to speak quickly,

"It's about time! We've been waiting patiently and thought you backed out on us!" the shrill voice penetrated the air making me wince.

"Dinotonians are honorable. We keep our word. I assume the preparations have been made and the matching program is operational?"

Sputtering, the man glared at me, "Yes the program is now running smoothly. All we need is the large sum of gems you promised us, and we can announce the program to the public."

I held back a growl that threatened to escape. Terrans were so greedy and pathetic. I had to deal with this particular one for months ever since my people first stepped foot on the strange planet looking for females to mate with. We had run the database of our old computer to it's limit scanning and searching for planets with compatible mates. The only planet that seemed to come close was this mud ball with a 95% compatibility rate. The terrans were aware of our presence of course, had even caught a couple of them trying to sneak onto our shuttle cars their government provided for us to travel back and forth.

At first there was full blown panic but panic quickly dissolved into excitement as they tried to get a glimpse at the new "aliens" on their planet. Thankfully the government was able to chase off the paparazzi and others. We made a public appearance and said we come in peace and all that, that we were looking for females to help us repopulate our planet. So, the matching program was born. After months of careful planning and preparation, it was finally ready for everyone. The program would match those who gave blood to their perfect mate and would be shuttled to our planet where they had seven days after courtship to decide to stay or go back to Earth. The men were excited and nervous about our program and admittedly, I was too.

"Are you listening?" the shrill voice cut through my inner musings making me wince again.

"Yes Mr. President, I'm listening. I will transfer the gems to your security when I appear this afternoon for my speech."

A wide grin split the mans face, "The announcement will be made this afternoon."

Turning off the device, I sunk into my chair rubbing my temples, "this better work." I grumbled to myself. A sound to his left made him spin around to face the intruder. I relaxed when I saw that it was only my advisor, Durkin.

"Sir, have things been put into motion? Everyone is very eager and want to know."

"Yes Durkin, everything is ready. I finalized everything with their President."

Durkin fidgeted, "So now what?"

I strode past him, "Now all we can do is wait and resume duties as normal." I said over my shoulder. There was no room for error, this had to work…or our species was doomed.

Outside awaited a shuttle car for travel and I shuddered. These things were so weird and foreign, it creeped me out. But it was for the good of my people. I squared my shoulders and signaled for my guards to accompany me.

Squeezing into one of these things was uncomfortable and the space was ridiculously small. Nevertheless, we all managed and sat in uncomfortable silence the entire ride to Earth's surface. The landing was unpleasant and jostled me too much for my liking, but I breathed a sigh of relief once I exited the shuttle.

Walking though the shuttle station, I noticed a crowd of terran women being held back by security officers. Some screamed in excitement, others yelled obscurities, most of them fainted. I tsked, such fickle creatures. How did that rust bucket of technology think that we were compatible with these defenseless and noisy fleshbags? My men were supposed to be attracted to these females? Ridiculous!

I moved purposely toward the podium in the middle of time square and tried to collect my thoughts. Just tell these terrans that the program is done, and you can return to the sanctuary of your planet, I reminded myself. Taking a deep breath, I stepped up to the piece of wood and was immediately bombarded with questions.

"Mr. King? What are you going to announce today?"

"Is the program done?"

"Do you feel justified taking away the choice for the women of this planet?"

"Will you ever leave earth alone?"

Growling low, I tried to get my anger under control, "people of Earth, we mean you no ill will and to answer a few questions, I am here to announce that the program is finally finished! We know that there are a lot of concerns for the women, but as it has stated before, a disease has wiped out ninety six percent of our female population. That is why we require the women to cooperate so my men can find their mate and we can save our species. I myself am not looking for a mate for personal reasons, but the women do get seven days to decide to stay with her compatible mate or return to Earth. We are simply trying to save our species and maybe find love. This universe is vast and until a few months ago, each of us never knew the other existed. So, I beg of you, can't we co-exist in peace?"

As soon as my speech finished, there was an uproar of more questions and accusations. I gripped the podium tight causing it to splinter. If the terrans weren't up to sharing their women or opening their mind to new experiences, how the Grekk were we ever going to co-exist?

NATALIE

      Oh my god! This was it. The program was finally ready. I stared at the TV screen in shock and horror. It was bad enough that they landed on our planet but what they demanded of us was appalling. Aliens didn't exist until a couple months ago, and no one really knew the details of the program the government was making. Now it was plastered all over the news and on every channel. And worst of all? It was mandatory. Most of the women on earth were excited and tried to get past the security to see them. She couldn't blame them, these aliens were super-hot with a capital H. Their dark skin ranging from different colors covered their muscled bodies and black scales covered them in most places. They had small spikes trailing down their back and their scaled tails continuously flicked back and forth as if searching for something. But what got them the most attention was that they looked more humanoid than anything.

I had to admit that their king that made the peace statement turned my head in interest, but he wasn't looking for a mate. I had not really heard much of what he said at the time, being too distracted by his rippling muscles and big bulge in his leather pants. But the one thing I did hear was he didn't want a mate. The sun had reflected off his crimson skin and dark scales making him seem almost God like. His deep green eyes felt like they were looking deep into my soul. But that was crazy. I couldn't deny that the king made me feel an ache in my heart…. and a coiling heat below the waist, but he had stated that he wasn't interested in a mate, and she wasn't interested…. was she?

No. Shaking my head I tried to clear my lust filled mind. I had a boyfriend, and I was happy with him. Ok, mostly happy. He had been getting distant with me lately and I was trying to figure out why. Tyrell was a handsome man with dirty blonde hair, chiseled chin, and ocean blue eyes, and of course all the girls were interested in him even though they knew he was in a relationship. Thirsty bitches.

There you have it folks! The program is done and now the question on everyone's mind, do these aliens come in peace? Or do they want to steal our women and enslave us?

The T.V boomed shaking me out of my thoughts. My heart did a little flip. The king sounded genuine when he pleaded to the crowd about coexisting. These aliens didn't seem to be the enslaving type. And in some small way, I sympathized with their plight and their struggle. Heat coiled in my stomach again making me wet as I stared at this handsome Alien. What would it feel like to run my fingers through that silky hair as he fucked me roughly against the wall?

"Snap out of it! You are taken" I scolded myself. But the heat continued to pulse between my legs and my heart refused to slow down. The king was hunched over the podium in defeat and my heart broke for him.

"The Galactic Matching Program intel's females are required to give blood to be tested and shuttled to our planet if you are matched by the computer. My men are very eager and will treat their match with respect and happiness. The courtesy seven days begin for the females once the shuttle car touches down on our planet. The men have in that time to try to win their matches affections. So, if you have been matched you are to report to the shuttle station immediately to depart. We do appreciate your time and patience."

There was a deafening silence as I stared gaping at the TV. Excuse me? We had to what!?!? There was no way I was going to the testing center for them to draw my blood so they could see if I'm matched to those aliens! It was mortifying the women didn't get a choice, that it was required! I watched as the king flashed a brilliant smile at the camera and wave to the gathering crowd of paparazzi. My knees went weak seeing his smile. Man, he could persuade even the timidest person to do anything.

A knock at my front door made me jump five feet. A pink flush covered my face as if I had been caught doing something naughty. Striding across the living room, I threw the door open to reveal my best friend, Bethany. She looked flushed and out of breath as she stared at me with huge eyes.

"D-did you watch t-the live announcement?" she gasped.

I nodded. My best friend and I were against these aliens forcing themselves onto our planet from the very start. But they did intrigue us. Blowing past me she sunk down onto the couch.

"It's required to get tested but there's no guarantee you'll be matched. I hear a lot of my college roommates talking about it. Some are saying they are going to get the testing over with and pray they don't get matched."

I thought of the king and wondered who he would be matched to since it was mandatory. A flash of jealousy stabbed through me and I jerked back in surprise, where did that come from? I didn't care about this stupid program and especially not the king. I would refuse the damn testing and hide out for as long as I could. It wasn't like the aliens would notice me out of the hundreds of women that would be tested every day. I would just bide my time.

"Women have already started to flood the testing center. It's honestly pathetic. I for one refuse to take part in any sort of testing. I say we go on the run."

I smiled, "how is it you know exactly what I'm thinking every time?"

She tossed her blonde hair over her shoulder dramatically, "because I'm awesome like that."

Giggling, I hugged her hard. I didn't know how I got so lucky to have such an amazing friend, but I was thankful. I ran upstairs and grabbed my suitcase. We would have to be quick and stay ahead of those alien assholes. The sound of a cellphone ringing made me pause. Bethany reached into her back pocket and took out her cellphone. She looked down at the caller ID and frowned.

"Who is it?" I asked nervously

"My mom. I'm sorry, I have to get this."

I gestured to the door and nodded. As she hurried out of my room I continued to pack. Being on the run wasn't going to be easy. But they had to try. Because I was not going to be forced together with an alien that a computer matched me with. I knew I had to pack light so I put only the necessities I would need in my bag. I was debating on bringing my coconut shampoo when a knock sounded on the door.

REXXOR

Being the first one to be tested was complete Grekking shit! But I had to show my men that their king was true to his word. Laying back on a medical chair in the testing center, I glanced around at the shiny and white décor that the humans used for all their medical facilities. Strange little creatures, but fascinating to learn about. I didn't want a mate and I was one hundred percent sure I would not be matched. I had a mate and I lost her to the disease. My heart tightened painfully in my chest. This was a huge waste of time and only duty kept me glued to the chair.

I drummed my claws on the arm rest of the strange chair impatiently. Where the *Grekk* was this doctor? The sooner I got off this planet, the better. Their customs were strange and weird to me. I heard the sound of quiet clicking before the door to the testing room opened. A woman who looked in her mid-prime entered wearing a long white laboratory coat and holding a needle.

"Hello your Majesty. I will be drawing your blood today so you can be matched."

I resisted the urge to growl in disapproval. That was a highly unlikely chance.

"let's just get this over with." I muttered.

Flushing a light color, the doctor shrugged and approached. Holding still, I tried not to gag on the overly sweet scent on this female. Why did she feel the need to smell like pollunated valassums? Was she trying to attract a mate? If so, she was going about it all wrong. After finding a vein, she plunged the needle in the skin triumphantly. She drew a little vial of blood and held a small fluffy white circle to my skin where she jabbed me.

"There we are. All done. You may go, call in the next person please." She chirped.

I left the white bandage looking circle discarded on the armrest. The needle puncture already healed.

"You will have results in the morning or sooner if you are matched!" she called freezing me in place with my hand on the doorknob. So soon? Shaking my head, I left briskly. It didn't matter, they would find no match.

Brushing by my men that were lined up outside the doctor's door, I tried to mask my emotions with a neutral expression. No matter what happened, I hope the men are matched. They are honorable warriors and deserve happiness. Climbing into the shuttle car, I began the long shuttle home. Touching down on my planet, two of my warriors greeted me.

"Welcome back my king" Nuthor exclaimed

"I assume everything went well on Earth?" Exxor asked at the same time.

Both warrior twins were identical and it was Grannthing difficult to remember who was who. Both had blue slitted eyes, long dark hair, and same blue colored skin.

"Yes, it went very well. The program is up and running and soon matches will be announced." I said walking at a brisk pace into my castle. "I am retiring to my chambers and wish not to be disturbed."

"Yes my king!" they answered in unison. I chuckled to myself, I feel bad for whichever mate they are matched to. Both of them seem like they would be quite the handful. I climbed up the stairs and opened my bedchamber door only to be met with a sickenly bitter scent. Grekk! Not her! Didn't she have anything better to do?

"I've been waiting for you my king." A voice purred behind me. I tried not to growl in frustration but failed miserably.

"What are you doing here Lillenth?" I made my way to my bed and laid down with my arm draped over my eyes.

"I thought I could help you unwind after such a stressful day seeing those disgusting terrans." She said huskily.

Maybe if I ignore her, she'll go away. It was when I felt cool air on my Duo cocks that I realized my leather pants were around my ankles. I sat up and glared at her.

"I am in no mood to do this right now Lillenth. I ask that you take your leave until I have need of you." I ground out, my anger flaring. She smirked and started to shimmy and shake in the traditional seduction dance. Her black scales raised and her red skin lightened to accentuate her arousal. She dragged a claw through her wet slit. Stalking over to me, she crawled up the bed and hovered over me with a hungry smile.

"Surely you want to bury your cocks in me so you can release that pent up pressure. You're not matched and with me, you don't need to be." She said reaching for my cocks and stroking up my shaft to the tip.

I grit my teeth and tried to think of anything that would make me go soft, but my traitorous cocks hardened with the need to find release. biting down my stomach, she wrapped her mouth around one cock and started sucking. I balled my fists and ignored the pleasure she was giving me.

"Relax my king, take whatever you want from me and find your release. It is an honor to serve you. I know you want to." She whispered.

Fine. She wanted me to release? Then I will use her as the whore she was. Grabbing a fistful of her hair, I forced her to deepthroat my cock. Gagging, she tried to pull away. Holding the back of her head secure, I slammed into her mouth again and again until her eyes were bugging out of her head and she was turning an ugly shade of blue.

Throwing her on the bed, I flipped her onto her stomach and raised her hips. Grabbing ahold of her tail I lifted her off the bed and buried one cock in her pussy and the other in her ass in one thrust. After several more thrusts, I quickly pulled out and spilled my seed all over her scales.

Trembling, she stared up at my wide eyed. Narrowing my eyes, I pointed a claw at her "You are a whore to satisfy my needs and that's it! Don't ever presume you are anything more or that I do not need a mate." I growled "now get out!"

She scrambled to grab her dress and ran for the door. When she reached the door she hesitated, "My King, why is it you never spill your seed inside me or giving me your claiming bite?"

Pulling up my leather pants, I gave her a hard look "I may never get matched, but my seed is for my mate and only her, as is my bite."

Looking at me thoughtfully, she nodded and shut the door behind her. I was finally alone. Laying back on the covers, I stared up at the ceiling. My eyes started to get heavy and soon I fell into a fitful sleep.

A high tinkling sound woke me from my nightmares of my ex-mate and it took me a second to remember where I was. Yawning, I wiped sleep from my eyes and trudged over to the holographic intercom where I received my messages. Yet another thing gifted to myself and my men during our first visit to Earth. I swiped opened the new message and looked at it in shock. I read and reread it and even pinched myself but no, I was not dreaming. There in big bold letters read,

Congratulations King Rexxor! You have been matched to Natalie Marina!

The grekking machine found a match? That was impossible! Even though I knew it was not possible, I found myself curious to know what my mate looked like. Swiping on the file attached to the message, I held my breath as I waited. When her photo popped up on the holo message, the air left my lungs in a rush.

She was breath taking. Her hair spilled down her back in waves and was the color of fire. Her skin looked creamy and my claws ached to feel how soft it was. But it was her eyes that held a spark of challenge that made my duo cocks stir. This female looked like a goddess. My goddess. For some reason the great gods above found me worthy to have another mate and I would not let this chance go.

Striding into my washroom, I tore my leather pants off and sunk into the stone tub. There was so much to do before I could meet my mate and I wanted to be presentable. As I rubbed suds over my muscled torso, my cocks stirred again making my imagination run wild. In my mind it replaced my hands with hers. In my fantasy, she squirted more scented liquid on her hand and washed my whole body until she got to where the V dipped in my waist, where my cocks stood hard and proud.

I moaned as she wrapped her lips around one of my cocks and fisted the other one. Taking me as far as she could into her hot mouth, she started to pump my second cock. Her rhythm moved faster until I shot strings of my seed onto the waters surface. I was still breathing hard from the powerful orgasm when a ping sounded another message. Washing away my seed, I got up and checked the new message.

King Rexxor, you have not confirmed if you accept your match. Please do so by swiping right to ACCEPT.

Of course, I had forgotten all about confirming that I wanted my beautiful mate. I had been so distracted by her that it didn't cross my mind. Swiping right, I quickly rushed back to the washroom to buff and polish my scales. I hope my mate found me worthy of her.

NATALIE

I stared in open mouthed shock at the message on the hologram device the security officer held out.

Congratulations Natalie Marina, you have been matched to King Rexxor.

I shook my head violently, "That's impossible! I never gave my blood to the matching center. This has to be some kind of mistake, a glitch or something!"

"Be that as it may Ms. Marina, it is standard procedure for you to go to Tyrannador and do the required seven days to see if you accept the match. Glitch or no glitch." The officer replied emotionlessly.

I balled my fists, "I will NOT go! It's not fair and I am not stepping foot on a shuttle car or on another planet for that matter until you redo the test!" even though I was furious, my heart sped up in excitement thinking about the handsome king.

The officers arm snapped out and grabbed my arm in a vise like grip, "It is not up to us mam, we are just following the rules." He said curtly as he started to drag me out the front door.

"NO!" I shrieked and grabbed on to the door frame with my other hand to halt the officers progress.

"Natalie what the hell is going on?" Bethany asked running into the living room and gasped. "What are you doing with her? Let her go! This is an outrage!" she yelled.

"Ms. Marina has been matched to the King of Tyrannador and it is required she go to their planet for seven days to either accept or decline the match. Now if you'll excuse me Ms. Marina" he turned to me, "we must deliver you to the shuttle car station."

My mouth went dry. This was not happening. It was impossible and I sure as hell was not giving in to a stupid alien king. Continuing to resist, the officer sighed and took out a syringe full of light blue liquid. I struggled harder as he plunged the needle into my neck. I slumped forward as my motor functions became more sluggish and was soon enveloped in darkness. Voices sounded around me as I became aware of the sounds of animal noises and unbearable heat.

"Why is she unconscious? Who did this to her?" A deep bass voice growled. The voice was above me and drifted like a caress across my skin making me shudder.

"She's stirring my King." Another deep voice to my left said. I cracked open an eyelid only to be met with harsh blinding light. Quickly closing it, I groaned and shifted my head to the side. Cool hands propped my head up as something was held up to my lips.

"Drink this little one. It will help." That same deep voice sounded making heat pool in my stomach. Blinking my eyes open slowly, two figures came into focus. My eyes met piercing dark green eyes that were filled with worry. The king himself was leaning over me and boy he looked even hotter in person. I shook my head and immediately regretted it as a sharp pain in my head made me see spots.

"Drink this." The king said shoving a waterskin up to my lips. I took a hesitant sip as the king stared. The refreshing liquid hit the back of my throat and I began to drink more deeply. Jerking it away, the king tsked "don't drink too much or you will throw up." I looked over to see two identical warriors with their arms crossed staring at me. I sat up and took in my surroundings. We were in some sort of a jungle with the sound of birds and other animals noises I couldn't quite make out. What happened with the security officer came rushing back to me making me gasp.

"Oh no! Please tell me that I'm still on Earth!" I looked from face to face wildly willing them to tell me I was. When the king shook his head my heart sunk. I can't be on Tyrannadon. I left Bethany and Tyrell back on Earth and they were probably hysterical when I was taken. The king frowned and studied me carefully before he got up and offered me his hand. I reached up and slid my hand in his as he helped me up.

A flash of soft golden light assaulted my vision, and a powerful sensation ran up my arm making me let go of his hand and stagger back. My panties were instantly soaked and my pussy throbbed to the rapid beating of my heart.

Rubbing my eyes, I looked up at the King bewildered. He was staring at the tattoos that spread across his arms and chest in shock and awe "you're the one" he whispered. His twin guards had their mouths open and eyes wide as if they've never seen tattoo's that glowed before. To be honest, neither have I until now. I snapped my fingers in front of his face that seemed to have a permanent awe struck look on it. Shaking himself out of his stupor, he straightened and looked down at me.

"Do you remember what happened? Why were you left out here unconscious?" he asked. I flushed and refused to meet his eyes. How do I tell the king of a planet I didn't want to be his match and freaked when I found out, so much so I had to be sedated? To tell an alien with such hope in his eyes that this match was a glitch in the system?

"I don't know." I stammered. His face clearly showed he wasn't buying it but he gestured for me to follow him as he and his guards moved deeper into the jungle. Without much choice, I reluctantly followed. After awhile, a huge stone castle came into view. This is where the king lived? The stone coloring was old and looked very impressive. As we got closer, I noticed a village below the castle where the folk were bustling and going about their day.

Walking through the village, vendors were loudly voicing their products and prices. I did a double take as I saw several actual dinosaurs walking about without a care in the world as the wandered from vendor to vendor seeking items to purchase.

It very eerily reminded me of the movie series Dinotopia. I loved those movies because dinosaurs could talk and were friendly. Apparently, it was all real. Except the dinosaurs that I could see were humanoid looking or carnivores. I couldn't see a single herbivore. It threw me off but strangely I felt safe surrounded by carnivores. As we got closer to the castle, I studied several vendors and found some items they were selling to be strange looking. One vendor was selling meat, another one jewelry, while others were selling bottles filled with weird looking liquid.

I neared another jewelry stand and slowed as a beautiful emerald necklace caught my eye. There was no way that was real, was it? "I see you have an eye for beautiful stones that would compliment your eyes." A silky voice whispered in my ear causing me to jump. I turned to see an older man with blue skin smirking at me.

"Oh I was just looking sir." He gaze looked me over and I stopped myself from shuddering in disgust. He leaned in close to the crook of my neck and breathed deeply.

"You are unmated." He stated with hunger gleaming in his eyes. What the fuck was he talking about? Mated? That sounded dirty and disgusting. I forced a smile to my face.

"Well thank you for allowing me to admire your stones." I said trying to get past him. Grabbing my arm, he smiled evilly, "you are allowed to admire and handle my stones anytime you want beautiful." His suggestive comment made me shudder and try to break free from his grip. The harder I struggled, the tighter his hold became. Before I could full out panic, I was wrenched from his grip and pressed tightly to a muscled torso. "How dare you attempt to attack the kings mate?" a low deadly voice growled. The man's eyes widened in surprise. I knew who it was before he spoke because of the soft gold glow that surrounded me.

"My King! I humbly apologize, I did not know she was yours. I was simply showing her the many stones I have to offer." He replied oily. I shivered and wrapped my arms around my waist. What a big fat liar! He knew exactly what he was doing.

Rexxor's arms held me tighter as he glared at the man "Byrnndr, you touched my mate threateningly, you are exiled to live far away from the village or the castle. When I make my morning round, I strongly suggest you not be here. If I see you again, your punishment will be execution."

Byrundr's mouth dropped open as he looked at Rexxor. his expression changed from shock to rage, "you can't do this! This was just a misunderstanding my king. I swear it won't happen again." He sputtered.

Rexxor gently pushed me in front of him and continued walking, "no" he growled, "it wont" I had to admit even I was shocked. That was possessive and ruthless of him. My nipples hardened and I suppressed a growl of frustration. Traitorous nipples! He talked about me like I was his property. I should feel disgust not lust. But heat coiled in my stomach as I remembered how it felt to be pressed up against his chest. I bit my lip and looked over my shoulder at him.

He was deep in thought but looked up as if he felt my gaze on him. His lips curved up in a small smile before he shook his head and fixed his gaze in front of me. My heart clenched painfully at that, and I didn't know why.

REXXOR

My blood still boiled as the image of that raptors claw on her arm remained fresh in my mind. He was trying to claim what was mine and it took all I had not to march back down the hill and rip him to shreds. My eyes drew back to my tribal tattoos and hope flared in my chest. She is my mate. I never thought I would get another chance at love or a family but here it was. Now all I had to do was win her trust and love.

I watched her hips sashay as she walked, and my cocks hardened. I let out a low frustrated hiss. She was perfect and here I was, close to spilling my seed in my pants like a damn young tyrannosaur. My mind strayed back to where I had found her unconscious in the jungle. Who would ever leave a female in the middle of nowhere and out cold? They must not treasure females like we do because she was far from the meeting place where the shuttle car was originally supposed to drop her off at. When she evaded to answer my questions fully, I knew she was hiding something. But I would let her tell me in time. For now, the clock was ticking and I didn't have much time to convince her to stay with me.

I would figure something out. She glanced over her shoulder drawing me out of my thoughts. My lips curled up into a smirk without realizing it and I shook my head to clear it of all the ways I would claim her on my bed. Keeping my eyes straight ahead, I tried to ignore the flash of hurt on her face. My chest constricted in regret for making her feel hurt. *I will make it up to her*, I promised myself.

As we entered through the entryway, a bitter scent I was so used to evaded my nose. I stiffened and braced myself for the inevitable.

"My king!" Lillenth's voice called out joyfully as she emerged from the shadows. "I am so pleased you have returned from that dreadful little planet."

"Lillenth. I appreciate you meeting me at the entrance, it saves me the hassle of trying to find you. I would like you to meet my mate Natalie." I said stepping up behind Natalie and putting my arm around her shoulders.

Lillenth's eyes narrowed at my arm for a minute before she turned to look at her in disgust. Natalie fidgeted as Lillenth looked at her up and down with growing distain. After a few minutes, Natalie held her hand out.

"Nice to meet you Lillenth, my name is Natalie." Lillenth stared at her outstretched arm for a moment then threw her hair back.

"Whoever you are, you won't be here long. The king doesn't need a new whore for his Harem, and you will never replace me as his favorite." She huffed before turning and stalking back down the candle lit corridor with her tail twitching.

I turned to see the mortified expression on my mate's face and silently cursed myself for not taking Lillenth's presence into account.

"Natalie, I can explain." I said. She held up her hand, halting my explanation.

"You are a king and are free to be with whoever you want. I'm glad that I know, it just makes my decision at the end of the week that much easier." She said emotionlessly.

Damn it! This was not going how I wanted it at all. Lillenth may have just grekked my only chance at keeping my mate. I made a mental note to retire her to the village as soon as possible. My shoulders slumped.

"This way, I'll show you to your room." I gestured for her to follow me as I continued down the corridor and up the marble staircase. Peeking over my shoulder, I see her looking around in awe. A small smile tugged at my lips as we climbed higher up. Would she like a tour of my castle? I could show her around and maybe she would forget the Lillenth fiasco.

Coming to a stop in front of the guest bedroom, I pushed open the double oak doors.

"This will be your room for the remainder of your stay here my lady." I said gesturing around the room. Her eyes grew wide as she looked inside.

"T-this room is for me?" she asked incredulously.

I chuckled, "Yes this is your room. I know it takes some getting used to, but I hope it is to your liking."

"Are you kidding?!?" she said with a wide grin, "This is the biggest room I've EVER stayed in!" I did a double take. Females on Earth were not adorned with jewels and worshipped? Well, that would change if she decided to become my mate. I will shower her with riches and worship the very ground she walks on every day.

"Thank you." Her voice brings me back from my daydreams of worshipping her jewel encrusted body to the present.

"A-anytime" I stammer "it was nothing. Only the best for you."

She flushes a light pink and I find it adorable. "well, I appreciate it your majesty."

Looking up at me, I suddenly find myself lost in her gaze. My body drifts closer to her like a magnet until we are inches apart. My hand reaches up unconsciously to stroke my claw gently down her chin and she shudders. She licks her lips and my eyes drop to her plump mouth. I find myself wondering what they would taste like and bend slowly. As if two magnets drawn together, she presses her body against mine as she draws her lips closer to mine.

A loud bang of the doors opening startle me out of my trance. Blinking, she flushes that cute pink color again and straightens her top. So close. The need to taste her lips linger as I turn and glare at the guard that interrupted what would have been a perfect moment.

"What is it?" I snap.

"My King! A fight has broken out between two villagers." The guard said solemnly.

Turning, I meet the icy glare of my mate. "It's fine, just go. I'm sure some girl from your Harem will warm you tonight."

Wincing, I turn and follow my guard out the door. Looking back as the doors close, I catch a glimpse of her with her head in her hands and her shoulders shaking. I ball my fists and force myself to keep walking, I want to take all of her hurt and sadness away. Walking down the steps of my castle, I vow that I will make it up to her and do whatever makes her happy.

NATALIE

What the hell was wrong with me? I never cried over any man and here I was crying that the man I was mated to, had a harem, crying for my best friend back on earth, and crying overall for having any connection to this king when my heart belonged to another. No matter what happened or how I felt, I had to get back to Bethany, Tyrell, and my old life back on Earth.

What was it about this alien that made me weak in the knees and lose all common sense? When I'm with him, I want to know all about him, including what makes him tick. I felt drawn to him like nothing I've ever felt before. Being around him was dangerous and if I had any hope of resisting him and going home, I had to keep my distance and wait it out until my time here was up.

Taking a deep breath, I dabbed my eyes with the end of my shirt. I could do this. Nothing to it. Good thing about being supposedly matched with the king? Access to everywhere and a huge freaking castle to explore. My inner adventurer pushed at me to explore every inch of this castle and I eventually gave in. Inching one of the doors open, I peeked out to see the corridor empty. I crept out and ran smack into a hard body. Hands wrapped around my waist to balance me. I looked up into the gorgeous face of one of the king's guards.

"Thank you. Sorry I rammed into you." I said in embarrassment

He bowed, "it's no trouble my lady. My brother and I have been asked to guard you while the king take care of village matters." His twin brother appears behind him giving me a friendly smile.

"I don't suppose you two would give me a tour of the castle?" I ask them batting my eyelashes. Looking at each other, they shrug and nod. Following them down the corridor, I take note of the different doors and other corridors. Wow. A girl could get lost in this castle if she wasn't careful.

As they show me the kitchen, throne room, and other various rooms, the adventurer in me squirms under my skin wanting to explore on our own. Making sure that they are looking ahead and talking among themselves, I slip down a random corridor and open the first door. The female I first met was laying on the bed playing with herself. I felt my face heat up in embarrassment as I tried to back away without making a sound. My foot must have scuffed the ground or something because the female sits up and pins me with a glare.

"I am so sorry to barge in like this" I said stumbling over my feet trying to backpedal "I must have gotten lost, and all the corridors look the same."

"Pathetic human. So clumsy and ugly." She hissed "why our king finds you attractive baffles me."

How rude! I thought as I looked down at myself. I mean, I may not be model thin or have the greatest complexion but that was no excuse to be mean. I open my mouth to tell her where to shove it but she cuts me off.

"As soon as the king realizes that I'm meant to be his mate, he'll dump your ass on that mudball you terrans call Earth and be with me forever." She sniffs haughtily.

Mate. there that word was again. What did it mean and why did that word place a warm and fuzzy feeling in my chest? No. She may be a complete bitch but she was right. I didn't belong here and I sure as hell wanted to leave as soon as the week was up. Man, why did that make my heart hurt? Shaking my head, I tried to focus on what she was saying.

"-never get rid of his Harem, he loves it too much. Especially me." Her gloating voice grated on my nerves.

"It's ok, he doesn't need to get rid of anything. Because I'm not staying." I said sweetly "besides, I don't want to fuck a man who may have diseases from his latest" I paused making it a point to look her up and down "conquest."

Snarling, she lowered herself into an attack position as I looked around desperately to find an exit. Just as I thought I was truly fucked, the wooden doors slam open, and the twin guards emerge. Breathing a sigh of relief, I walked behind them to put distance between me and crazy pants.

"What is the meaning of this?" one of the twins boomed, his voice echoing off of the stone walls.

"This terran barged in here and tried to attack me!" The female on the bed shrieked pointing an accusing claw at me.

My mouth dropped open, what the hell was this woman's problem?

"Are you crazy? I got lost and opened this door and found this chick basically fucking herself." The guards shifted uncomfortably at that but I didn't care. "She harassed me and told me that I wasn't the kings mate and that the king doesn't want me. Which is fine by me because I'm not staying when the seven days are up. She was right about one thing." I claimed giving her my best scowl "I don't belong here."

Gesturing in front of them, the one on the right cleared his throat "best to leave what conspired to the king. Do not worry, he will see to it that the behavior of Lillenth is taken care of."

Nodding, I walked out the door and threw a smirk at her over my shoulder. I knew it wasn't smart to egg that crazy woman on, but she was bringing out the inner bitch in me. As we walked, one of the twins stayed behind me as the other one led the way. The silence was both awkward and weird and I had to break it with any small talk I could.

"So I know you two just saved my butt in there, but I don't know what to call you two to thank you. I'm sure I can't just call you Hey you! Or Thing one and thing two."

The one behind me chuckled as his voice vibrated through the corridor "I am Exxor and my brother is Nuthor. I am sure you have noticed that we are twins. We hatched together in the same nest. Both of us are from the Velociraptor tribe."

I mulled over the new information in my head as we walked. Velociraptor tribe? That was probably why they had blue skin. But why were the carnivores not ripping each other's throats out? They seemed to co-exist peacefully. Was their king a velociraptor too? As I went over all the questions in my head I smacked into a back of solid muscle. Nuthor grabbed my waist before I fell, and I flushed with embarrassment.

"Sorry" I mumbled as I got my footing. Looking anywhere but him, I tried to act casual.

"It's ok Natalie. Accidents happen." I jerked in surprise.

"You know my name?" I asked incredulously

"Of course, we know your name. Our king was so excited to learn he was matched with you and talked non-stop about you and your beauty." He said amused "it was both sweet and annoying."

Exxor chuckled as he ran his claws through his hair "what do you think brother? Will we be matched to a Terran?"

Nuthor smirked, "I'm not sure she can handle both of us." They both laughed.

Wait. Both of them? "Are you saying that you two will be sharing a mate?"

Nodding, Exxor spoke, "we thought a lot about it and when we were giving blood, we mentioned that our match should be told that we are a package deal and that she be ok with two mates."

Well then, good luck to the poor girl they were matched to. Smiling I continued to follow them back to my room. I hope they got matched, I may have known them for a short period of time, but they seemed like great guys and deserved to find love.

REXXOR

Oh, for the love of everything! Will everyone just stop fighting? I thought with annoyance as I broke up a velociraptor and Dilophasuras from drawing blood.

"Woah, break it up! What is going on?" I yelled to be heard over the angry screaming of the two fighting. As if just realizing I was there, they both awkwardly bowed. I raised my eyebrow "well?"

An old man pointed accusingly at another elderly man "Your highness, this despicable animal tried to steal the meat from my basket that I was trying to pay for."

"I was not stealing from you, you took it out of my hands when I tried to put it in my basket you thief!" the other barked.

An uproar of angry words drowned out what I said so I raised my hand above my head until everyone quieted down. "It matters not who took what from who, can't we split the steak in half and be on our merry way?"

"But my king, this is the last steak and it's not enough to spilt it so we can feed our families."

Turning, I pinched the bridge of my nose in frustration. How did I expect us and the terrans to co-exist when I could barely keep my kingdom from falling apart? I placed my hand on the old man's shoulder, "keep the steak and feed your family. I will dig into the emergency supplies to acquire meat to help the other's family."

Dropping to his knees, the velociraptor took my hand and kissed it "thank you my king! You are truly a great leader."

Funny, I didn't feel like one. My people were starving and there wasn't enough game on our planet to go around. We were barely scraping by and that made me feel like a failure as their king.

"Go to supplies and grab some meat for this man." I whispered to one of my guards. He nodded and took off towards the castle. Turning to the elderly man I clasped his hand gently "my guard went to grab some meat for you and your family. I will stay with you until they get back."

Tears filled his eyes as he shook my hand "bless you my king, bless you."

Smiling, I guided him gently to the side and under the shade. I cared for my people and it hurt to see them suffering. I would figure something out, I had to. There was a lot of things I had to fix. Natalie's face flashed in my mind as I waited for the guard to return. Leaving her had been the hardest thing I ever had to do, but I left my two best guards with her. I would trust them with my life. They were great men and even better friends. We may be different species, but we became very close after my orientation as king years ago. My father had died from a horrific battle a year before the disease wiped out most of our female population, including my mother. I swallowed around the lump of emotions lodged in my throat as I composed myself.

These terrans would fix a big part of my kingdom's problem and while this program ran, hopefully I would be able to fix the other problems that plagued my kingdom. The program was still so new, and it worried me that things might go wrong. But so far, things were running smoothly. After all, the program brought me her.

Natalie. I thought dreamily. Her fiery hair made me want to run my claws through those silky locks, her lips just begging to be tasted, those curves that accentuated her body that would make any man drool, and her green eyes that freeze me in place and make me want to get lost in them. She was the whole package and man did I want to unwrap her slowly. Watch her eyes cloud over in desire as she moaned my name in pleasure. Imagining what her slit would taste like made me drool and my cocks harden painfully in my leather pants.

Walking off to the side where no one could see, I quickly adjusted myself so my cocks weren't making a tent in my pants. A flash of blue caught my eye as it turned the corner making me pause. There wasn't very many velociraptors in the village and the one I talked to went home to his family. *Was it Byrunndr?* No, it couldn't be. If he knew what was good for him, he would be long gone. I flexed my claws and growled, it would be nice to remove his head from his body myself, but no one disobeyed an order from their king. Byrunndr was too much of a coward to disobey me, especially if it meant his certain death. My guard came running up shaking me out of my thoughts. Taking the meat from his outstretched hand, I gently placed it in the elderly mans hand.

"This should be enough to feed your family tonight. The market should get a fresh supply of meat tomorrow. I will be joining the hunting party myself."

Clasping my hand, the man bowed and gave me a teary smile, "bless you my king."

Helping him off the busy walkway, I held him up until he was able to hobble off to his home. These were good people, they were just under a lot of strain with every growing problem. Problems I needed to fix, and I intended to fix them all. Starting with this Bride program and leading the hunting party myself tomorrow morning. There was not a lot of game, that left the herbivores over on the far side of the jungle. We had a fragile peace treaty with them but if it came down to it, I would do whatever it took to keep my people alive. If that meant breaking the peace treaty so that my people wouldn't starve, so be it. I've lost too many people already, I'll be damned if I lost anyone else.

A mouth watering scent wafted over me and I turned to find where the delicious aroma was coming from. Natalie was coming down the steps of the castle with the twin guards rushing to catch up. As soon as she saw me, her face brightened for a second before she bit her lip and looked away. Meeting her halfway, I looked down into her dark green eyes. *So the aroma is coming from her* I mused as I stared at her. She smelled like honey with a dash of vanilla. This must be what others meant when they said their female had an appealing scent only her mate would be able to smell and would continue to smell more delicious until fully mated. Once mated, the smell would be there, but bearable. It was getting more difficult not to take her right then and there, but I bit my tounge and smiled.

The twins ran up out of breath, "I'm sorry my king, she wanted to see the village again and-" Nuthor exclaimed

"she's super fast for a terran." Exxor finished.

"Is that so?" I asked looking down at her smirking face.

Tossing her hair over her shoulder, she scoffed.

"Of course it is. You call yourselves dinosaurs? Couldn't even catch me."

I bent down so my lips were by her ear.

"In our true form, you wouldn't be able to stand a chance little one. I would catch you and watch you squirm beneath me." I whispered, "In either form I would watch you squirm as I licked and sucked your wet cunt, moaning my name."

Her heart rate increased as her breath quickened. Taking her earlobe in my mouth, I nicked it playfully with my teeth. A soft whimper escaped her as she presses herself against my chest. *Grekk!* I cursed as my cocks hardened and my fangs extended. A throat clearing snapped me out of my lust haze to find we had an audience. Pushing away from me, she flushed and straightened her shirt.

The twins, having witnessed and heard everything, were looking anywhere but me. The villagers had gathered to see what the commotion was, and I bit my lip. Her intoxicating scent still surrounded me, and I wanted to back my mate up against the stone wall and claim her lips in front of everyone. I took in deep breaths to calm down and found that to be a mistake. Sucking in deep breaths made her scent fill my lungs and nose and I knew I had to get out of there before I did something that caused her to hate me forever.

"I have urgent business to take care of and wish not to be disturbed." I announced backing away from Natalie and her mouthwatering aroma. My cocks strained against my pants as I turned and fled to the privacy of my castle. My fangs lengthened more as if to search out and pierce Natalie's soft neck.

I tried to clear my head of my beautiful and luscious mate but by the time I arrived at my chambers and closed the door behind me, it had gotten much worse. Her scent still clung to me, and I rushed to the washing room to wash it off before I lost my mind with desire. When others had talked to me about the mating frenzy and intoxicating smell their other half produced to drive them crazy until they mated, I had laughed thinking they were just being dramatic. But experiencing it for my own, I wasn't laughing anymore.

Chucking my pants and jumping into the stone tub, I scrubbed my skin raw trying to remove the smell that was my mate. But even with chaffed and raw skin, I still smelled her as if she were right next to me. Groaning, I looked down at my hard Duo cocks in frustration. Well, if I wanted to face Natalie again, I had to relieve this pressure, even if for a short time.

Grabbing hold of my cocks, I started pumping a slow rhythm. I pictured her face as I imagined her wet in the tub with me. Her damp hair clinging to her face as she looked at me under her lashes. Her breasts bouncing as she drew closer to me. Biting her lip that she always seemed to do that drove me crazy. And then I would gaze into those green eyes that held a spark of her fire and would darken with desire around me. My rhythm became short and choppy as I franticly chased my release, envisioning my perfect woman. Her name spilled from my lips as I came harder than I ever had before. As my cocks shot strings of my seed everywhere, I sank deeper into the tub, limp with pleasure. Coming down from my orgasm, I stared up at the ceiling. This woman could destroy me with just her delicious aroma and a sexy smirk. In a nutshell? She was trouble, and I was beginning to fall for her. *Grekk!*

NATALIE

My mouth hung open unattractively as I watched the king run away from me and my chest tightened. Had I done something wrong? *Guess I was wrong when I thought he wanted me* I thought glumly as I picked my fingers-a nervous habit. Standing up straight, I squared my shoulders and curled my hands into fists. It was good he didn't want me, it made it much easier for my decision at the end of the week. Besides, I had Tyrell. A boyfriend who loved me and didn't run away from me like a coward, who spoke his mind. A boyfriend who…hasn't tried to get in contact with me since I was taken from Earth. My heart sank as my shoulders slumped. Where was he and why hadn't he tried to visit or contact me?

There were no rules about visiting someone who shuttled to Tyrannadon, were there? What was it about me that made men run for the hills? Man what was wrong with me? Was I really worried about Tyrell and what other men thought of me? Bethany would scoff at me and tell me to get my shit together. My smile slowly disappeared as I thought of my best friend. She had to witness me being drugged and manhandled out of the house. I hope she was ok.

"Miss Marina?" A deep voice startled me out of me inner musings "If you'll follow us, we shall escort you to dinner with our king. It has been prepared and will be served upon your arrival at the table."

I had forgotten about thing one and thing two. Nodding, I walked towards the castle and the kings face popped up in my mind. He is so handsome, with his high cheekbones and a body sculpted by the gods. I blushed and tried to put the sexy king out of my mind but failed miserably. Trudging up the stairs, I wondered what his bedroom looked like and if he had a big bed. Many things flew through my mind including rumpled sweaty bedsheets and a hard shaft in my mouth.

My mouth watered thinking about what Rexxor must taste like. A yelp shot out of my mouth as the stone floor came up to meet me and I frantically pinwheeled my arms to slow my fall. Face planting on the ground, I refused to move due to extreme embarrassment.

"Natalie! Are you alright?" a deep bass voice boomed causing me to shudder and bite my lip. Looking up, I see the king rushing down the corridor towards me.

Stooping down, he gathers me into his arms and picks me up. Holding me close to his muscled chest, he looks down at me with eyes filled with worry. Him holding me like this makes a gooey warmth expand in my chest as I look into his slitted green eyes that seem to hold the key to my soul. Unconsciously, I reach up and brush a strand of his hair from his face. Sucking in a sharp breath, his eyes look at me with intense heat that a blush works its way up from my neck and flushes my face and my thighs are instantly wet with my arousal. He takes in a deep breath and his eyes widen in shock for a moment before he leans in close and nibbles my earlobe.

A shudder of pleasure runs through me as my mind becomes incoherent and the need to have him inside me replace all thought. As if remembering where he is, he jerks his head back and gently puts me down. A pang of disappointment shoots through me as I try to fix my shriveled appearance. Clearing his throat, he offers his arm to me and I loop my arm in his as we walk to the dining hall. We walk through two big wooden doors and Rexxor stops.

"I can escort her the rest of the way to dinner." He says looking over at the twin guards "stay outside the doors and I will yell if I need you."

Nodding in unison, they close the doors behind us, leaving the both of us alone with each other. Picking at my nails, I distract myself by studying the room. Stone pillars surround the room and there is a huge, long table in the middle of it. Cushioned red seats and jewels adorn the chairs and a surprised gasp escapes past my lips as I look closer at them.

"Are these real?" I ask incredulously.

Pulling out the chair I'm looking at so I can sit, he looks at me quizzically.

"Yes, they are real, why wouldn't they be?"

I blush and chew my lip nervously, "well it's just that it's rare to find gems like this on Earth and they are very expensive if sold to the right person." I stammer.

Holy shit! Did I just say that to the king? Stupid! I can't believe I just told him that he could sell the priceless stones in his chairs to people on Earth. Mortified, I quickly sit down and hide behind my hair. Chuckling the king sits across from me and I peek up at him through my lashes.

"It's ok love, I have come to an understanding that Tyrannadon gems are quite…. valuable on your planet. Right?" he asks studying me.

I nod and he smiles. My heart stutters and my knees become weak. *Good thing I'm already sitting down* I muse to myself as I try to steady my jackhammering heart.

"If it would please you mate, I could gift many gems to your people." My heart melts and I find myself smiling.

"You would do that, for me?" I ask "what about your people? Don't they need them to trade or make jewelry?"

Shaking his head, he smirks "our planet has so many of these stones, that they won't be missed. You couldn't throw a rock on Tyrannadon without finding one."

Well now that was interesting. Maybe before I left here, I could bring some back with me. As soon as the thought crossed my mind, my heart clenched painfully. Did I really want to leave? *You haven't been here long and don't plan to stay!* I chastise myself. I would stay the necessary week and leave as soon as possible. I would not lose my heart to the king, I couldn't betray Tyrell like that no matter what I felt for Rexxor. Throwing up walls around my heart, my face hardened.

"That's nice. But we are in a dining hall aren't we? Are you so rude as to not offer any food to your guest?" I quipped. A flash of hurt crossed his face and I refused to feel guilty for it. After all, this bastard landed on my planet and demanded that my people save his species. If I reminded myself of that, I wouldn't do anything stupid. Like imagine if his lips tasted how he smelled - like cinnamon. Composing his face to a neutral mask, he clapped his hands, the sound echoing throughout the room. The doors at the other end of the room – most likely connected to the kitchen – opened and several men came out with silver platters.

One placed a crystal goblet in front of me and poured red looking liquid into it. Another put a platter of what looked like a pink steak down by me, but I was too busy staring at the servers. They had black scales and their skin was the iridescent color of purple. Their slitted eyes looked silver, and I ducked my head as one of them caught me staring. Bowing to the both of us, they filed back into the kitchen. Huh. Wonder what that was about. Picking up my silver fork, I poke at the meat wearily.

"What kind of meat is this?" I ask avoiding his gaze.

"We have a peace treaty with the herbivores and in that treaty, they agree to give us their dying, dead, or sick members to nourish us so that they remind safe from us. We also hunt other animals in the jungle." He says with an edge to his voice, and I couldn't help but look up at him.

Tearing his eyes from me, he starts cutting his steak. Following suite, I cut my steak in several pieces from I stab one with my fork and pop it into my mouth. Spice and smoked flavor burst on my tongue, and I moan in delight. His eyes snap to me when I moan, and his eyes are like molten lava.

"It's so good. The chef was really good at combining the flavors." I said around another bite of steak. A drop of the steak juice drips from my chin and lands on the top of my breast. It leaves a trail before it disappears in my shirt. A crunching sound makes me look up and I'm shocked to see the king hunched over the table with his hands gripping the wood table so hard that his knuckles are white and the table splintered.

"Your highness, are you alright?" I ask, moving to get up. Holding up his hand, he signals for me to sit back down.

"I'm fine." He replies in a husky voice. His body is trembling and his breathing deepens "Let's just finish our meal and I will escort you back to your chambers."

Shrugging, I eat the last of my steak and cautiously sip my drink — which tastes remarkably like berry limeade. The king was affected by juice sliding down my cleavage, but why? Was his reaction…arousal? Needing to find out before dinner was done, I waited until he wasn't looking before I spilled the rest of my drink on my breasts. Jumping up, I grab a satin napkin and begin dabbing at my chest.

"Crap, I'm so sorry Rexxor! I wasn't watching carefully. Clusty me!" I exclaim carefully studying his reaction.

His eyes widen and he squeezes his eyes shut. He stands up so fast his chair clatters to the floor and I have a clear view of his boner. My own eyes widen, and I have to bite my lip hard to focus my thoughts from not going in the gutter.

"I-I'm so sorry Natalie, but I'm afraid I won't be able to accompany you to your chambers. I need a lot of things I need to take care of." He gasps turning and fast walking to the doors. From the looks of it I'd say taking care of his hard member was on the top of his to do list. I watched him throw open the doors and talk quietly to his guards before disappearing down the corridor. Sighing I put my napkin down and turn to find the guards approaching me.

"Ms. Marina, the king has asked us to escort you safely back to your chambers. May I ask-" Nuthor began.

"What happened in here?" Exxor finished and I couldn't stop the smirk curling up my lips.

"Well boys, I was a klutz and spilled my drink on me. Stupid me right?" both smiled knowingly before turning and leaving the room. Playing with one of my curls, I decided to ask them my question before I chickened out.

"So you guys know the king pretty well right? Why is he always acting weird towards me?"

Exxor turns to look at me with confusion, "what do you mean?"

Looking down, I shuffle my feet "well he's always trying to put distance from us and when I think he's not interested, he touches me and I feel a spark. Then right when we are about to kiss, he turns and runs away from me. What is that about?"

The twins look at each other before answering "you felt a spark with our king?"

Nodding, I wonder why they are looking at me with awe.

"The marks glowing are just the first step. The next step is feeling like that person you can't live without and their smell is irresistible." Nuthor explains carefully.

Well shit. Marks? Check. Can I live without him? Crap, my useless heart was saying no and my mind was screaming YES! I swallowed hard. I found him to smell pleasant but not irresistible. Maybe I wasn't his and he just thought that.

"Natalie. When a dinosaurs marks glow, it indicates that you are mates. And dinosaurs-"

"Mate for life." Exxor finishes.

The wind whooshes out of my lungs in a long exhale like a punch to the gut. I shake my head as I hear my heart pounding in my ears. That's not possible. These idiots believed in love at first sight basically. That's insane! *But what about what you feel for him? And his marks only glow around you* the small voice in the back of my head mused. This wasn't supposed to happen. I was supposed to wait out my week here and go home, not become someone's mate. I mean, the matching program had glitched, I couldn't be his mate.

"I can't be. There must be a mistake." I squeaked.

"All the signs are there my lady. We even recognize it in our king." Nuthor said.

"I don't find his smell irresistible! So there's a sign missing." I say triumphantly.

Exxor scratches his chin in thought "Maybe terrans don't have that sign like our people do. So our king must be experiencing that one by himself."

I cock my head confused, "what sign is that again?"

Gesturing for my to walk ahead, they take the formation in front and behind me. As we walk, Nuthor explains more.

"Well for our people, we go through the three signs until we fully mate. And even then, the signs never really go away, just dull a bit. When a male finds his mate, his marks that he is born with from his tribe will glow and he will experience a powerful and addictive smell coming off of his mate. And the urge to mate will become stronger until you two become one. After that, your addictive smell will linger but won't be as powerful."

I stare at him dumbfounded. I was making Rexxor go crazy being around me by my smell? Huh, that wasn't something you heard every day. Coming to a stop in from of my room, I thank the guards and close the doors behind me. God this was a lot to process. Glancing over, I spot the stone tub and perk up. Maybe relaxing will help. Turning on the water, I strip out of my clothes and sink into the hot water. Turning over the events from today, I start rubbing a sweet smelling liquid all over my body. Once I am all clean, I lean back and float in the water. Maybe I was too hard on Rexxor. I mean, he didn't ask to be mated to me, it just sort of happened. Tomorrow I would request to get in contact with Tyrell and assure him that I was coming home. I had to get home or I would want to stay. *Well fuck!*

REXXOR

My mates scent still engulfed me as I woke at the crack of dawn. *Grekk!* I had tried to take care of my throbbing member several times last night and I seemed to get impossibly harder each time I came. The conversation from dinner last night flashed in my mind and my chest tightened when I saw her Stoney expression. *That's nice. But we are in a dining hall, aren't we? Are you so rude as to not offer any food to your guest?* Her words echoed in my head like sandpaper, and I winced. Her warm personality had been replaced with uninterested detachment in an instant and somehow, I knew it was my fault. I shouldn't have pushed and tried to kiss her. Nor should I have whispered those things in her ear. But her smell, it did something to me and made me rash and bold. I knew what I wanted, and I had thought she wanted me too, but after last night, I wasn't so sure.

Throwing the covers off me, I rushed to take a quick bath before slipping on my pants. I had to focus if I were to lead the hunting party this morning. Looking over at the connecting wooden door that led to Natalie's room, I balled my fists. I wanted to check on her, but she didn't know that her room was connected to mine so I could watch out for her. For the rest of her stay, she wouldn't know so that I didn't freak her out even more. She deserved her own space so that she felt safe. Leaving my room, I strode down the corridor and out the front entrance. Hurrying down the steps, I walked toward the gathering crowd of hunters at the edge of the jungle. When they saw me, the men bowed.

"Good morning my king."

"How are you this morning?"

"Hope all is well with your match."

"We weren't informed you would be joining the hunting today your highness."

Well wishes and questions sound around me as I stand in the middle of the gathered men.

"I know it is last minute, but I will be leading the hunting party today. So, stay focused and when you find a herd, hunt prey, or get hurt, signal the rest of us with your inner voice so that we may assist you."

Everyone nodded and started stripping. After I stripped my own clothing, I joined my men in shifting into my true form. Breathing deeply, I squished the mud between my claws. It felt great to be in this form, I felt more like myself. Turning my massive head, I looked around at my fellow carnivores.

Remember what I said everyone! Stick together unless you find a herd then signal if you need us. Now move out! I project out to them and get murmured agreements before we move as one into the jungle. Once we get further out, we slow and quiet our steps to hunt. Walking slowly, I step over fallen branches and crouch down to examine Tomorah tracks in the dirt. Bending lower, I sniff at the tracks. These are fresh, barely an hour old. Growling low, I shuffle forward. Since it was an hour old it wouldn't have strayed too far.

Men, I scent a Tomorah! The tracks aren't that old, so I think it or the herd isn't too far away I claim looking around.

Another tyrannosaur steps besides me growling, *I scented it too my king. There is a clearing ahead and that's most likely where the herd is.*

Jerking my head behind me, I nod to everyone *you guys hear that? Follow behind me in formation and wait for me to give the attack signal!*

Getting to the clearing's edge, I crouch low and take in the herd scattered around in the tall grass. Tomorah are big, furred animals that when taken down, could feed my people for weeks. But you had to be careful not to get gored by their sharp horns on their head. We had hard scales, but our underbellies were soft and exposed. The trick was to single one or two out of the herd and attack as a unit. Crawling forward a few more feet, I spring up and charge, letting out a battle roar. Knowing that was the signal, the men charge out from the trees and run towards the herd. Stalking the edge of the herd, I try to nip a few of their legs to change their direction. The herd is thin and has been hunted to almost extinction by my men and I, and as I circle the herd, I worry. If the herd is this thin, it won't be long until they have been hunted to complete extinction. One breaks off from the herd and I run after it, leading it towards my men. As the twins cut it off from escaping, I lunge forward and grab it by its throat. With a quick twisting motion, I snap its neck and drop it dead at my feet.

A dark green Tyrannosaur barrels by me and scoops my kill from the ground and swallows it in 3 bites. Letting out an angry roar, I butt him with my head making him stumble and fall.

YOU IMMBECILE! THAT WAS FOR THE VILLAGE! WHAT THE HELL WERE YOU THINKING? I glare at him. The others look at him with a mixture of shock and rage.

Wincing, the Tyrannosaur bows his head *my king, I am so sorry! I let myself get so overcome with hunger that I didn't think!* He says laying down at my feet in submission. Growling in frustration, I try to think of what to do. A dilophosaurus steps forward and bows.

My king, if I may speak, I have a thought he hesitates as if waiting for permission. I nod at him, and he speaks in a rush *I know we have a treaty with the herbivores, and they are under our protection, but look around your highness, the game on our planet is extinct or nearing extinction and there are a lot herbivores to tide us over for months. It will give the game in this jungle time to produce and multiply so we have plenty of meat. I know it's a hard choice to make my king, but we have been talking and it makes sense.* He finishes his rant, bows, and steps back.

With a heavy heart, I nod. He was right. With very little game on Tyrannadon and my people desperate, I had to make the hard decision.

Very well. But if we are going to do this, we play it smart. Which means we do it MY way. Do NOT move or do anything unless I tell you to. Gather around me and pay close attention to the plan I growl. As the others gather around me, I shoot a glare at the Tyrannosaur that put us in this mess.

You go back to the village! I bark *You have done enough for today. And if I see you again today, I swear to the goddess above that I will kill you. So, I suggest you make yourself scarce for the rest of the day until I have need of you.*

Bowing his head in defeat, the Tyrannosaur turns and shuffles through the vegetation and out of sight. Thumping my tail on the grass, I shake my head in irritation. He cost us food for my people and I had to make this right, even if it meant breaking the treaty my father before me carefully put in place. I didn't want to do this, the herbivores I had met seemed like good people, but I had no choice. Supply was thin and I needed to save my people. Sighing, I turned back toward the men, *walk carefully men and with stealth. If we are going to pull this off, we need exact precision and grace. Stick to the plan and we may just get away with this. Move out!*

Walking towards the front of the pack, I wondered if this really was a good idea. Herbivores were smart and always by each other. Not to mention their village was ten times bigger than ours. They had more people and more resources. They were flourishing and we were struggling. If you looked around, it made sense why they were a flourishing community. They even had their own King. I growled low in my throat, personally I think this planet should only have one leader but there wasn't much I could do. These veggie munchers owed us for protecting them all these years, and we were going to collect. As we got closer to the herbivores village, we crouched down and studied the layout. Kids shrieked as they played outside the gate and some herbivores had shifted to munch on the grass lazily. Being in your true form just to stretch your legs, I could relate to. It felt like it had been too long since my last shift and I was thrilled to feel the leaves and mud in between my clawed toes again. As I watched, the kids chased each other back inside the village's gate and the herbivores slowly shifted and left toward the village one by one until there was one Triceratops left eating the grass. Pushing aside the pang of regret, I snuck forward until I was behind it. The plan had been divide and conquer but they had basically just served this herbivore to us on a silver platter.

Lurching forward, I sank my teeth in its tail and yanked it back towards the shelter of the trees. It immediately started thrashing and making keening noises. Grekk!

Everyone, change of plan! We need to hold it down and snap its neck before it draws the attention of the other Herbivores! I send out frantically as I try to hold on to the squirming Triceratops. My men jump into action and surround it as I try to hold it still. Wrapping my tail around its leg, I lay it flat so the dilophasarus and Exxor could slit its throat. But it's thrashing too much, and we can't get a clear killing shot. Darting out of the trees, the tyrannosaur I sent away comes barreling towards us. What the Grekk was he doing?!? Before any of us could move to stop him, he bends down and cleanly snaps the herbivores neck, silencing its distressing cries. Licking at the tangy blood on my mouth, I look from the dead animal and back to him.

Why did you help us? You had orders to stay away! I snarled as he bowed.

I felt awful for eating our last kill and causing you to resort to hunting the herbivores. I wanted to make things right and now, its blood is not on your hands. I made the killing blow to make it up to you and to beg your forgiveness my king.

I curled my lip as I sized him up.

Well I guess you did prove yourself useful. You will help us gut it and clean the meat to bring back to the village.

Nodding, he shifted and turned to join the others. It took us some time cutting through the armored flank with our claws and the sun was setting when we were done cutting and cleaning. Bending over my burlap sack, I looked inside appreciatively. It was a nice haul and each of our sacks were overflowing with meat.

"My king, what do we do with the body? Do you think they'd suspect us?" A Nuthor asked, wiping his claws on a cloth. The acidic scent of his fear hung in the air and I nodded.

"Probably. But with the treaty in place, they won't have any proof. They may just think it's a rouge. There are many around here. But we should take the body with us just in case." Shifting, I crouched and picked up the carcass with my teeth.

I will need one of you to carry my sack with yours since my mouth is already full. I project, focusing on not dropping the body. Without the meat and it's internal organs, it felt much lighter, It was just awkward to hold onto. Picking up my burlap sack, the velociraptor bowed and followed the path back to our village. Stomping forward, I let my mind wander. Am I proud of what I just did? No. But it had to be done. I wouldn't have had to take such drastic measures if it hadn't been for that grekking idiot! He may say that this dead beasts blood wasn't on my hands, but the moment I made that horrific decision, all the herbivores – including the one we killed - blood stained my hands.

Nearing our village, my nose picked up that mouthwatering and addictive aroma.

Natalie. I shook my massive head and tried not to stumble from how overpowering it had become. It seemed in my true form; it was ten times worse. My saliva glands were working overtime as I searched for my mate. We were almost to the gate, and I became lightheaded as her scent engulfs and teases me. Walking through the gate, I see her instantly rushing down the castle steps towards me with a beaming smile on her face. All my instincts are screaming at me to mate her right here in front of everyone, but I squash it down as I step forward. She slows down as she nears me, her eyes going wide as she stares at me open mouthed. It takes all my strength to keep my cocks from coming out of my mating pouch and standing to attention. As she gets closer, I struggle hard not to envision one of my cocks in her open mouth and her hand fisting the other one.

NATALIE

Holy balls! it was an actual fucking dinosaur right in front of me! I slow as I notice the dead animal in its mouth. What on earth happened? Looking down the line of carnivores, I see they are all holding bulging sacks that are dripping blood. The carcass in one of the Tyrannosaurs mouth looked like a Triceratops and I covered my mouth in horror. Didn't they have a peace treaty? Dropping the animal at it's feet, the Tyrannosaur stepped forward.

I can explain everything Natalie a deep voice vibrates in my head making me yelp. I look around wildly, "who said that?" I gasp.

It's King Rexxor, I am the dinosaur in front of you. Don't be afraid, I will not harm you The Tyrannosaur says bending close so he can nuzzle my hand. The words I want to say won't form due to shock and I just gasp at him open mouthed like a fish out of water. I should feel terrified, but I'm not. But that could just be because I'm going into shock. I could feel my heart racing and the world slowing down.

I know this is new to you and may come as a shock, but everyone on Tyrannadon is a shifter. There are our true forms, which we are standing in front of you with, and our other forms that the goddess has granted us with to better communicate with others, prosper, and attract a mate. We have never been mated outside our species and I didn't quite know if you would be able to hear my inner voice, but apparently you can. Knowing you can hear me proves you are my mate

No matter what I do I can't seem to stop gawking at the king. I knew they were dinosaurs and I heard they were shifters but hearing and actually seeing it was an entirely different story. I was standing in front of creatures that my planet though died off millions of years ago, and to see them flourishing and on a different planet, well it was downright incredible. Stepping forward nervously, I raise my hand.

"Can I touch you?" I ask. Without warning, he pushes his muzzle in my hand and I yelp again. Get it together you scaredy pants, he won't harm you I assure myself. Taking a deep breath, I run my hand from his mouth and down his side. I trace the scales down his tail and a shudder runs through him. His scales must feel sensitive if he's in this form. Feeling a bit bolder, I stroke his underbelly. A low growl vibrates his chest and I pause. He sounds kind of like a purring cat I chuckle to myself and I begin to trace the spikes down his back. Noticing a rather large sack between his legs, I reach out and poke at it. A strangled whimper falls from his mouth and his body starts trembling. Yanking my hand back I run around to his head.

"Oh my god Rexxor I'm so sorry! Did I hurt you? I swear I didn't mean to!"

It's ok mate his voice sounded strained in my head *what you touched was my mating pouch where my…. members are*

I look at him confused for a couple of minutes before realization dawn on me. Oh god, I just basically handled his dino balls. Shit. Wishing there was a rock I could crawl under, my face heats up and I refuse to look at him.

Natalie, it's ok to be curious. But for future reference, just your touch on my sack will force my…ahem…members to come out He stammers.

Looking down, I notice that he's right and two huge pink dinosaur cocks are standing ram rod straight. Flushing a darker red, I avert my gaze and squeeze my thighs together to keep my sticky arousal from seeping down my legs. Rexxor's nostrils flare as he breaths in and his eyes lock on mine. He probably smells that I'm horny, damn his heightened sense of smell! A dinosaur getting a boner shouldn't be making me hot, but here I was. Doing a double take, I check again to see that there are in fact two cocks. Wait, two cocks? What the hell was the other one for? Or was that just in this form?

"Can I ask you a...personal question?" I ask biting my lip nervously. Bobbing his massive head up and down, the king inches closer to me.

"Why do you have two cocks?" I blurt out, then realizing what I've asked, I hide my face in my hands as heat flushes my face. Gathering the courage to peek at him between my fingers, I see what looks like a shocked expression on the Tyrannosaurs face.

He growls low – his equivalent of a throat clearing – and thumps his tail on the ground.

Well Natalie, when a dinosaur finds his mate, he claims her by making love in....all her holes he hints as his scales flush a darker red. Realization dawns on me again and my eyes are as wide as dinner plates. He had to put one of his thick massive cocks...in my ass? Oh god! I knew he meant in his other form, but even then I saw the massive outline of his junk through his leather pants from time to time. How the hell were both of those supposed to fit inside me? Imagining those cocks filling me up made me bite back a moan. They never mated with humans before, and it was possible he would tear up my insides, but what a way to go.

Natalie, are you alright? I detect your heartbeat has increased Rexxors deep voice growled in my head. Yeah and I bet he could just smell all the lady pheromones coming off me too. Licking my lips nervously, I nodded. His eyes immediately locked on my lips and his gaze darkened. Growling, he examined my body appreciatively. Oh I couldn't let the opportunity to tease him go, so I cocked my head and shimmied my hips a little. Turning away, he stood stock still.

"What's wrong your highness? Cant take a little temptation?" I teased.

Shifting too quick for my eye to follow, his arm circles my waist and he roughly pulls me against his chest. My hands splay across his impressive pecs as his other hand raises to fist my hair.

"Oh my fiery mate, you are more than just a little tempting. But I am not the only one effected here, am I?" he purred and bent to nip his teeth teasingly on my ear. Gasping, I arch into him and throw my head back as his nipping kisses leave a sizzling trail down my throat. Taking a deep breath, his fist tightens in my hair.

"your scent just keeps getting stronger Natalie and soon, I don't know if I will be able to stop myself." He kisses the other side of my neck, making my skin feel like its on fire. I can feel his hard cocks pressed against my thigh and I bite my lip hard.

"s-stop yourself from what?" I manage to gasp out.

Stopping, he pulls away and looks deep into my eyes, "claiming you"

My nipples instantly hardened and my pussy throbbed. Damn he was good. It was getting harder and harder to avoid him.

"what's stopping you?" the words left my lips before thinking and I wished I could shove them back in my mouth.

His jaw tightened as he studied me for a moment. Reaching up, he brushed a strand of my hair behind my ear.

"I will not claim you unless you ask me to. Until you are begging me to sink my cocks into you and moan my name." he whispered, causing goosebumps to raise on my arms. Smiling sweetly, I leaned in to lick his pointed ear.

"I promise you I won't cave in that easily big guy. I'm the type of girl that will leave you breathless and wanting more. By the time I'm done with you, you'll be begging for your release." I reply huskily.

His arm tightens around my waist as a shudder rips through him.

"We'll see little one" he murmurs "lets head up to the dining hall for dinner. Its getting late."

I blink and look around as I realize he's right. The sky lit up with light pinks and dark oranges as the sun sank lower in the horizon, and the village folk had seemed to disappear to give them privacy or to go about their lives. What the hell was wrong with me? I wasn't the type of girl to tease and get groped out in the open. But around Rexxor, I felt like a completely different woman. A very horny woman who didn't care about getting caught with her pants down, who wanted to climb the king like a tree and kiss him hard as she yanked his hair in her hands. Yep, she was absolutely and utterly fucked. Trying to still her fast heart, she reached for his outstretched hand. Walking hand in hand, we walked towards the castle and I let my mind wander. I missed my best friend terribly and I hoped she was alright. If she were here, she would've slapped me silly for getting enamored with Rexxor, and slapped him for good measure. Chuckling to myself, I climbed up the castle steps. Rexxors thumb gently caressed the top of my hand as we continued down the corridor to the dining hall. It felt nice but my stomach churned as I peeked up at the handsome man. I knew I couldn't lead him on because of Tyrell back on Earth. I had to cut it off before it got too serious, that was the right thing to do.

But if it was right, then why did my heart squeeze painfully at the thought of leaving him? Steeling myself, I asked the question before I lost my nerve.

"Do you have a hologram communication device?"

He froze and I held my breath as I waited for him to answer.

"Yes I do. Your Government gifted me that strange device when we first came into contact with them." His tone held a frosty edge to it. Oh boy, he was not going to like what I had to ask next.

"why?" he asked sharply and I faltered. Gathering my courage, I decided to just come out and say it.

"Well your highness, I was asking because I would like to contact my boyfriend and check in."

He furrowed his brow confused, "what is a boyfriend?"

Fuck! Was he really going to make me spell it out for him?

"A boyfriend is someone your close to and share your intimate thoughts and feelings with. Someone to occasionally make love with…" I answer fiddling with the hem of my shirt, refusing to look up.

The silence stretches on for so long that I finally look up at him through my lashes. The look of hurt and pain makes my breath catch in my throat.

"You….have a mate?" his pained whisper echoes around us.

"yes" that one worded answer seems harsh coming from my lips.

As if my answer makes up his mind, his face hardens into a steel mask of anger and he balls his fists so hard that his claws puncture his skin and blood drips from his fists. In this moment, he looked like an avenging fallen angel from hell and there was nothing I could do to stop him. Snapping his arm out, he grips my wrist and drags me down the opposite end of the corridor where the steps going up to my chambers are. Stumbling behind him, I don't say a word. I know he needs time to process this. Arriving at the door to my chamber, he releases me and turns to leave. Anger coils in my gut and I grit my teeth.

"So that's it?" I shout "your going to throw a bitch fit because I actually had a life back on Earth? Well excuse me your royalness for not being excited about being ripped from my planet and dumped in this shithole!" I bow mockingly "or not being ecstatic about being your mate and not immediately putting your cock in my mouth like you expected! Earth women are not easy and will not bow to the likes of you!" I scream and point at him accusingly.

"Besides, I don't know why you try so hard to fuck me if you have a harem at your disposal." I snort "you have a crazy ass dinosaur chick who says she's going to claim you for herself anyways."

Rexxor spins and slams his fist into the wall beside me causing rubble to rain down on my head.

"oh I'm sorry princess that I'm trying to save my people from dying out. So sorry for having my fathers harem basically thrown at me when he died. I keep those women in the castle so that they have somewhere to stay! Without me they have nowhere else to go. Lillenth is a mistake that I should not have kept repeating and I'm sorry that I had to make hard decisions like killing a herbivore, while the treaty was still intact, just to feed my people. But most of all, I'm sorry that I ever fell in love with you." He snarled. His words were like a slap in the face and my lip trembled.

"I didn't ask to be here! I never gave my blood and your stupid program glitched. Being manhandled, drugged, and stuffed into a shuttle car to follow your damn protocols was over the line and fucking barbaric!" well there it was, the truth was finally out. Rage glittered in his eyes but I refused to back down.

Spinning away from me, he walked briskly into the darkness.

"You'll get your precious contact call." He called over his shoulder "you won't have to worry about me bothering you for the rest of your stay here. When the seven days are up, I suggest you be on that shuttle car back to Earth."

It felt like my heart was being torn in two as I slid to the floor, buried my face in my lap, and wept.

REXXOR

    Red clouds my vision as I thunder down the corridor, her sobs still ringing in my ears. She had a mate this whole time and still decided to play with my heart? Who the Grannth did she think she was? I looked down at my royal tribal marks in disgust. I had let myself believe she was specifically matched to me, and the goddess above had deemed me worthy of a second chance at happiness. But it seemed like the goddess had a sick sense of humor. I couldn't be with a mate that didn't want me. Bursting through the front entrance, I strode down the moonlit path. My hands throbbed from my claws piercing my skin, but I didn't care. I had to get out of here and clear my head. Running at a full sprint, I slipped out the gate and headed towards the jungle. I leapt over a shrub and shifted mid jump. My clothes shredded and I landed hard on my clawed feet causing the ground to shake. Following the path my pack usually takes towards the clearing, I stalk forward angrily. Reaching the clearing, I paced back and forth snarling.

My heart was shredded and it felt like there was rock sitting uncomfortably in my stomach – crushing and sinking lower until I felt completely numb. She wanted to go home so badly? Fine. I would request a shuttle car after call so she could be with her mate and people. I will leave her alone until she departed my planet, maybe then I would be able to nurse my broken heart in peace. Because I knew in her presence, I would wilt and give in to her. Around her, she could ask for my soul and I would give it to her. But she already had both, and somewhere deep down, I knew she still had my heart. Even if she left Tyrannadon, a piece of myself would go with her.

Shaking my head as if to rid myself of any thoughts of her, I started to sprint through the trees. Hunting always seemed to help and it would get my mind off of her for a while. Backtracking to where my men and I saw the Tomorah herd last, I shuffled forward quietly, avoiding large branches and pressing my feet deeply in the soft dirt to prevent alerting the herd to my presence. A flash of movement from the corner of my eye had me freezing in place. Ducking down low to the ground in the shadows, I watched a velociraptor dart out of the trees and into the tall grass. The grass shifted as the dinosaur snuck quietly towards the sleeping herd of Tomorah. Who the Grekk was this animal and why was it ignoring the trees we marked as our territory? Even with this part of the jungle marked by my men and I, this velociraptor didn't seem to care. Growling softly, I watched the mystery dinosaur move with grace as it snapped the neck of a youngling and drag it into the grass. It was obviously a male, but why did his scent smell familiar?

As I tried to piece together who this guy was, another Tomorah – a bit older than the youngling that was killed – wandered by me to graze on a lush patch of greenery. Lurching forward, I wrap my mouth around its neck and quickly snap the hairy beasts neck before it can cry out. Shifting, I bend over it naked and began the gutting. By the time I am done and have a good haul of meat beside my resting on a leaf, it's early morning. Rolling my head to the side and cracking my neck, I glance around to find something to carry my haul in. Finding nothing, I walk over to a nearby tree and shimmy up it to grab a couple huge leaves. On the ground, I begin to weave together a pouch to put the meat in. After two hours, I pile the meat in my makeshift pouch and shift back into my other form. I take a minute to stretch my sore muscles before I gently grab the pouch between my teeth and run back to the village. As soon as I am past the gate, her scent hits me like a bag of rocks.

Skidding to a stop, I see her over by a stand that is selling jewelry. It's the same stand she stopped at before when she first arrived, but of course, with a different person behind the stand. She's looking down at the same emerald necklace that had caught her eye in admiration. Her long hair spills over her face as she takes a closer look and my heart skips a beat as the morning light rests on her hair, causing it to shimmer and making her look like a goddess. *Mine!* The thought rises in my head possessively. Bending to put the pouch on the ground, I shift and stand there, watching her. Against my better judgment, I start to walk over to her. I couldn't help it; it was as if a compelling force were dragging me over to her and there was nothing I could do to stop it. As if sensing I was there, she straightened and turned to look at me. Surprise passes her face as she sees that I am nude then darken with desire. Grekk! *You can do this* I tell myself *just act casual and walk by her.* But my legs stop when they are next to her and I cant seem to tear my gaze from hers. Her eyes keep flicking down to look at my cocks and I have no doubt that they are already hard for her.

"your highness, it's good to see you." She stammers as a flush works its way up her neck and reddening her face. She tries to keep her eyes locked on mine but they kept straying down. I bite back a chuckle and hold myself back from stroking my claw lightly down her cheek. Forcing my face into a neutral mask, I nod.

"I assume you slept well?" I ask as I pretend to study my claws.

"Yes, I slept as well as can be expected." She mutters looking away. My stomach recoils in regret but I push past it.

"I have given it a lot of thought and have decided to let you use the communicator when I hail your government for….business." I hedge. There was no need to let her know that I was calling to request a shuttle car to take her home tomorrow. Beaming, she looks up at me.

"Thank you Rexxor! That is very thoughtful of you, and I appreciate it."

I grit my teeth and ignore the way my heart squeezes painfully at the joy on her face from being able to talk to her mate. Watching her put the necklace down, I have the sudden urge to buy it just to see that smile light up her face. I bet it would look absolutely breath-taking adorning her neck as I worshipped her naked body. I bite my tongue hard enough to taste blood as I call on all my strength not to crush my lips to hers and explore her luscious curves. Turning abruptly, I walk quickly towards my castle. My hard cocks bounce as I stride through the entrance and towards my bedchambers. It wasn't smart to shift without bringing a backup pair of clothing or shredding my clothes mid shift, but I wasn't thinking, and, in my anger, I had completely forgot. Though the look on her face when she saw me naked, was worth it. That look proved to me that she desired me too, that the mating bond was affecting her too. My cocks throbbed at the memory of the look of desire and her lips parting slightly, forming an O when she was surprised. Leaning against the wall, I grabbed a cock in each hand and squeezed to find some sort of relief. Unfortunately all that did was shoot pleasure though me and make them impossibly harder. Stroking my shafts with quick precision, I thought of Natalie. Her soft kissable lips and the way she felt pressed up against me, the way my name sounded perfect on her lips. Closing my eyes, I pictured her in front of me and taking one of my throbbing cocks into her mouth. Her sucking and licking until I felt like I was about to explode onto her warm waiting tongue. A sharp gasp echoed in the corridor and my eyes snapped open. I see Natalie looking down at my cocks in horror. Confused, I look down to see Lillenth with bock of my shafts in her mouth. Where the Grekk did she come from? I thought it was all in my head, I didn't know that someone was actually sucking me off.

"Natalie, I can explain." I reach out towards her. Backing away, she puts her hand over her mouth, her eyes filled with unshed tears. Spinning, she runs the other way until she's swallowed up by the shadows.

"GREKK!" I roar and shove Lillenth backwards. Glaring down at her, my hands itch to claw her eyes out "What do you think you're doing?"

Smiling, she sits up and runs a claw gently down my shaft.

"I'm showing you that we are destined to be together. You weren't meant to be her mate, I was. That tiny terran will never be able to take all of you. You'd rip that poor girl apart" She purrs. Considering her words, my heart sinks. She's right. My mate seems far too petite and delicate for me to the bonding with. If I hurt her, I would never forgive myself. Groaning, I put my head in my hands. Why must the goddess above be so cruel? Raising my head a bit, I stare at my royal marks. They wouldn't have glowed around Natalie if she wasn't my mate and incompatible with my anatomy. Stepping back, I shoot Lillenth a glowering look.

"My royal marks glow when I'm around her and her scent drives me wild with lust. She is absolutely my mate and very compatible for me. Do not assume you are my mate when your very smell makes me want to throw up and I can't stand being around you. Natalie is kind and you are a treacherous snake! GUARDS!" I yell.

Nuthor and Exxor burst from around the corner, spears raised.

"Yes, my king?"

"What do you command?"

Pointing at Lillenth, I draw myself up straighter "escort Lillenth to the village and move her into one of the houses, make sure she has everything she needs, but I want her out of my sight now!" I bellow.

Grabbing her arms and yanking her upright, the guards march her down the corridor while she screams and curses. That takes care of that problem. Now I had to find Natalie.

NATALIE

Drawing in deep shuddering breaths, I lean against the wall and try to blink the tears away. So much for Lillenth being a mistake that he never wanted to repeat again. I'm such a fool! And here I thought that he was actually a great guy. But like all men, he had just wanted to get into her pants. Mate or not, I was not staying here when my time was up. Thudding footsteps made me wipe my eyes quickly and straighten the short dress I was wearing. Thinking that it would distract the king from his anger so I could apologize for hurting him, I had worn it hoping my plan would work. But now I didn't care. That asshole deserved every word I said! I refuse to bow to a man who is a player and I will shield my heart from him.

Turning a corner, his face showed his relief as he jogged up to me.

"Natalie, I have to explain. Lillenth was being-"

"No, it's ok." I cut him off "We aren't together so it makes sense that you should find your release elsewhere. You don't need to explain anything. A king can do what he wants and take whatever he feels like right? I mean, that's what you did, so it must be true."

His eyes glitter with rage and he opens his mouth probably to spew more bullshit, but I cut him off again.

"I have already made my decision that I will not be staying here after the seven days are up. I reject the match. Now if you'll please show me to where your communication device is, I would like to check in with my boyfriend, who actually gives a damn about me and doesn't spout lies."

His jaw clenches as he balls and un balls his fists. A touch of fear creeps in my mind but I push it away and hold my ground. Finally, his shoulders slump and he motions for me to follow him, then he turns and leads the way down the corridor. Stopping by a door that's right next to my chambers, he looks over his shoulder at me.

"These are my chambers. I put your room next to mine to protect you." He whispers as he pushes the door open. A warm feeling spreads through me at his words. No! I refuse to feel flattered that he basically put me next to him to keep an eye on me. Stomping over to a small table at the edge of his bed, he picks up a strange circular device. As he fiddles with it, I look around his room. It's like mine but with a huge bed with red satin covers and pillows. Gold trim covers the edge of the covers and a big window with a carved in cubby to sit on is at the other side of the room. His bathroom has two tubs that are already full of water and I'm instantly jealous. I'd love to have two tubs! His room smells like pine trees and cinnamon, so essentially, it smells like it. Making sure he's not looking; I draw a deep breath into my lungs and just breathe him in. His smell both calms me and makes me wet. Damn it! The last thing I want is for him to smell my arousal.

Finally figuring it out, he holds it up triumphantly.

"I will hail your government and you can take it from there." He says, gently handing me the device.

"What about your business with the government?" I ask curiously.

He shrugs and picks at his claws "I will do my business after you're done."

Chewing my lip, I nod "Ok, so how do you hail the government on this thing?"

Plucking the device from my hand, he swipes at it and turns it on. The screen projects in the air between us as he slides it right and clicks a red button. An image of the president pops up on the screen as it starts ringing.

The balding man appears on the screen looking surprised.

"Well, isn't this a surprise. What can I do for you Mr. Rexxor? The program is fully functional and there are no take backs on the gems you gave us." His shrill voice raised suspiciously.

"Mr. President, I am calling on behalf of my…. mate." he hesitates before the word mate and my heart lurches. "She requests to speak to her mate to check in as she calls it."

"Mate? I thought you were her mate." the president sounds confused as he looks from me to Rexxor.

"Excuse me for interrupting, but I'd like to get in contact with my boyfriend Tyrell." I say refusing to meet the king's eyes and keeping my eyes glued to the president.

The president nods and starts playing with his device "I will patch you over to the Boreman's household right now. We made sure that every home had a device so the program could be more effective in receiving alerts and messages." He replies.

A few minutes later, his face disappears and is replaced with a calling symbol. Shifting from foot to foot, I continue to look anywhere other than Rexxor. Suddenly Tyrell's mom's face pops up. She looks confused and is close to the camera where I can see up her nose.

"Stupid thing, can't work this damn technology." She mutters then finally puts it right side up "Oh Natalie! It's so good to see you, Tyrell and Bethany have been worried about you nonstop!" she exclaims.

I smile, it was good to see a familiar face "Hi Mrs. Boreman, is Tyrell home? I'd love to check in with him and let him know I'm alright." The camera shifts at a weird angle before she appears again.

"Of course, dear! Your friend Bethany has been coming over every day since you were taken to make sure my Tyrell is ok. Poor girl was so shaken up." She says as she walks up a flight of stairs. At the end of the hall, she stops to open his bedroom door. What I see inside makes my heart stop and tears blur my vision. Bethany is naked and on top of Tyrell and in the throes of ecstasy as she rides his cock. A scream sounds around me, and it takes me a minute to realize its coming from me.

I can't move and my throat is raw from screaming, but I can't tear my eyes away from the betrayal in front of me. Bethany looks over her shoulder and her surprised look turns into one of horror as she tries to cover herself. Tyrell is looking at me in disbelief with his mouth hanging open.

"You son of a bitch! With my best friend?" I scream at him as sobs pour from my throat "all this time I thought that you couldn't get ahold of me, and you were trying everything you could do come see me."

He looks at me with guilt written all over his face as he pushes Bethany off him.

"Natalie, I am so sorry! It was a moment of weakness, and it won't ever happen again. She means nothing to me!" he stammers as Bethany shoots a glare at him.

"Save it asshole!" I yell "I can't believe I held myself back from getting to know a really sweet guy because I wanted to be loyal to you! I felt guilty for wanting to kiss him before I caught him with his whore and now, I know something very important. Men are pigs even if they are a different species! You both can go to hell!"

His mom comes onto the screen and starts hitting him with her purse and yelling about something to do with loyalty and clean sheets but I'm too mortified to stay.

Spinning, I storm furiously out of the king's room and start to run. As tears stream down my face, I run blindly until I find myself at the bottom of the stairs. Running out the front entrance, I run down more stairs before making a beeline towards the jungle. If no one wanted me and always were treating me like shit, then I would live by myself in the jungle. Hell, maybe if I got lucky enough, a rouge carnivore would put an end to me and put me out of my misery.

REXXOR

I stare at the door Natalie ran out of in shock. Her mate had broken the sacred bond we Dinotonians hold dear. Turning back towards the image still on the screen, I glare at Natalie's supposed mate.

"What are you looking at bastard?" the terran male barks, his eyes narrowing.

"I'm looking at a poor excuse of a man who doesn't and has never deserved a woman like Natalie. You are pathetic and should be ripped apart for your betrayal." I snarl.

"If I recall, she did also say she caught you with a whore. Now who's being a hypocrite?"

I recoil as I think about his words. As much as I hate to admit it, he's right. I may not have intentionally sought out Lillenth, but it's my fault for not kicking her out of the castle to begin with.

"You don't care about her, and your actions claim you never have."

"Oh, and you do?" he asks sarcastically.

As soon as the words leave his mouth, I realize I truly do care about her, and that I always will. She has managed to get under my skin no matter how hard I tried to stay away or tell myself to not care.

"Yes." My one-word answer makes him do a double take as he studies me.

"I did care for Natalie at first, I really did. But I started to develop feelings for Bethany and things kind of took off from there. When Natalie was taken, I made my move."

He waited for her to be gone before he went after Bethany without telling Natalie how he felt? He felt sick to his stomach. This grekking idiot was just begging to have a death wish. Leaning in close to the camera, I gave him a menacing look.

"You are lucky that we are on different planets you disgusting piece of grannth! If you try to contact her or try to visit my planet, I will kill you. It won't be a quick; I will draw it out until you are begging for death." I growl threateningly before crushing the device in my hand, cutting off the live feed. I should be worried about losing connection to the terran government, but in this moment, I don't care. I had to find Natalie. Racing through the corridors, I try to catch a whiff of her scent but fail. Running by the stairs, her scent wafts to my nose.

Taking a running jump, I launch myself in the air and land at the bottom of the stairs. Her scent comes from outside as I follow it to the edge of the jungle. Oh no. Her being in the jungle by herself without a trustworthy dinosaur by her is dangerous. Shifting, I run into the jungle at a full sprint. If anything happened to her I would never forgive myself. *She has to be ok* I think as I frantically try to smell her aroma, *or I will hate myself forever.*

NATALIE

Running through the jungle, I wipe at my eyes furiously. I don't know where I'm going, I just know that I must get away from the village. Space to think and figure out what I'm going to do. Stopping, I put my hands on my knees and catch my breath. *Man, I was not built to do track and field* I thought as I drew in deep breaths. A shrub moves to my right, and I eye it wearily. It may have not been the best idea to run into the jungle without a dinosaur escort, and I may have wanted a rouge to kill me, but I didn't now. Emerging from the vegetation, a man I had hoped to forget smiles evilly at me. This cannot be happening! I thought the king banished him from the village! I turn to flee but ran smack into Lillenth, who was coming at me from behind. This can't be how it ends. I refuse to let it be.

I feign to the left and dart right when Byrunndr takes the bait. Before I've gotten a few feet, a claw entangles in my hair and yanks me back. A stinging pain shoots through my skull and I scream. Lillenth slaps her hand over my mouth and leans close to my ear, the foul stench of her breath making me gag.

"You're not going anywhere you whore. And when we dispose of you, the king will have to see that we are meant to be together." She snarls.

The faint scent of cinnamon lingered on her lips making my blood boil. The image of his cocks in her mouth forever burned in my mind.

"You can keep him." I spat "you two deserve each other. I want nothing to do with him." She smiled sickeningly and tsked.

"The king has feelings for you despite your ugly appearance and he will always love you unless you are dead. Imagine how distraught the king will be once I tell him his beloved mate was murdered by a rouge carnivore." She plastered a look of concern on her face as her eyes filled with tears.

"My king! I did everything I could, but I was too late to save her!" she wailed.

Even though I hated this bitch, she was pretty damn convincing. Wiping her eyes and smirking, she tightened her hand over my mouth.

"And when he's so upset, I will be there to love and comfort him. Help him get over you. Then he'll see he was wrong about his bond with you this whole time." She snickered. Balling my fists, I swing at her fat head, but she moves out of the way. Stupid dinosaurs! My life was perfect before I met them. But being here also uncovered my lying ass boyfriend, so I guess that's a plus.

Twisting my arm behind my back, Lillenth marches me towards Byrnndr. Struggling, I try to break free a hand darts out and slaps me across the face. My head snaps back from the force of the blow and my cheek stings.

"Stop struggling disgusting terran." Byrrndr snaps and looks over my shoulder at lillenth "gag her so she doesn't alert the king where we are. And tie her hands and feet while you're at it."

Throwing me on the ground, she binds my hands and feet and stuffs a rag that smells of feet in my mouth. It even has a tangy taste to it, and I swallow the bile that rises in my throat. Tossing me over his back like a sack of potatoes, Byrnndr strides through the trees while lillenth trails behind him. After what feels like forever, he stops at a door that seems to be carved into a grassy hill. Getting some serious hobbit vibes from this place, but frolo wasn't coming to rescue me and I was screwed. I was the shiny ring that was about to get tossed into the lava pit.

I wanted to yell out, "don't do it frolo! The ring is your precious!" and laugh at the confused faces of my captors, but I couldn't say a damn thing with this gross rag in my mouth. Byrnndr bent to enter the hobbit hole in the hill and my head slammed into the top of the door. Ouch. What a dickhead. Throwing me down, I was cushioned on a bunch of furs on a mattress. *I usually get to know a guy before I'm tossed on his bed* I muse dryly as I watch the big oaf drop a bag he was carrying. The place is one big room, but cozy. Dirt walls, a couple logs where a campfire was burning before, and stockpile of wood for said campfire. Grabbing a longer piece of rope, lillenth ties me to a wooden pole in the middle of the room. After tying me up, she turns towards Byrnndr and fingers the straps of her makeshift dress seductively.

"Now that she's been taken care of and wait for the king to come find her, I know of a way we can pass the time." She purrs and I roll my eyes. These dumbasses better not start fucking each other or all bets are off on not puking. Shimming and shaking in some sort of a weird ass dance, she slowly walks over to Byrnndr and starts stripping. Completely naked, she gets on her hands and knees to pull his pants down. His cocks spring up and harden. Nope. I was not watching this. Turning my head, I squeeze my eyes shut. Even though I couldn't see anything, I sure as hell could hear it. The sound of moans and slurping went for a couple minutes before it was replaced with flesh slapping on flesh. Gross! Did these fuckers have no decency? Trying to drown out the sounds of my captors having sex, I think of Rexxor. My heart ached picturing the handsome king. I said a lot of hurtful things to that man and all he did was act like a gentleman. Well, sort of a gentleman. My face heated up thinking of his dirty whispered words and his claws gently gliding over my lower back. A stab of guilt shot through me as I recalled my harsh words and the hurt look on his face. *God I was such a bitch* I thought glumly.

All he wanted was a mate and thought the computer had matched us. I led him on and didn't tell him immediately about the glitch. My shoulders slumped as I bowed my head, I wouldn't blame him if he didn't bother to save me, I deserved this. I lashed out to Rexxor because I was afraid of my growing feelings for him. Because in the short time I've known him, I've fallen hard for the kind king. I jerked my head back in surprise, I loved him. Now that I've admitted it to myself, a lot of things started to make sense. Like how hurt I felt to see Lillenth suck him off, and how pissed I was when that bitch said I would never be Rexxor's mate. I bit my lip to choke back a sob and my heart sank like a stone. I was never going to see him again and I had so much to tell him. I had to apologize to him and tell him I accepted the match. There may still be four days left, but I already knew the match was accurate, glitch or not. All I had to do now, was escape. I risked a peek over at my captors and instantly regretted it. Byrnndr was balls deep in Lillenth and eyeing me hungrily. I shuddered in disgust and tried not to puke. I may not be a virgin, but I wanted my first time with a dinosaur to be with Rexxor. Forcing myself to smile, I crooked my finger to beckon him over. The velociraptors eyes flashed, and he quickly pulled out of his skank. He strode towards me, and it took everything in me not to shrink back at his menacing approach.

Sitting up tall, I fiddled with the straps of my shirt and gave him a meek shrug and a small smile as I held up my bound hands. Bending down to untie me, his eyes stay glued to my chest where I've made my cleavage prominent.

"What the grekk are you doing?" a shriek sounded, and I knew without turning that it was Lillenth. Blinking slowly like he was coming out of a trance, he paused. But it was too late, the rope binding me lay in a pile at my feet. Jumping up, I slammed my knee high and smiled when it connected to his ball sack with a satisfying crunch. Doubling over, he wheezed and gasped as I darted towards the door.

I skidded to a stop when I encountered a pissed Lillenth blocking the entrance.

"And where do you think you're going you grekking whore?" she hissed.

Feigning right, I ran to the left to get around her, but she grabbed a fistful of my hair and yanked me back hard. My scalp stung and a pained scream forced its way past my lips. Dragging me back, she tied my whole body to the pole. Sitting up and holding his injured balls, Byrnndr glared at me.

"You grannthing whore!" he growled "I will teach you not to mess with a dinosaur that is superior to you in every way."

His first blow, hit me in the stomach and I gasped. As he continued to beat me, I tried to curl up in a ball but was bound too tight. My throat was raw with screams that spilled out of my mouth like a painful chant. My ears started ringing and I grew lightheaded as I tried to see out of my swollen eyes. An enraged roar came from outside making the blows stop. *That sounded like Rexxor* I thought dreamily as my body throbbed. That wasn't possible, Rexxor was back at the castle.

"What is he doing here?"

"How the grekk did he find us? He's not supposed to find us right now!"

My captors were firing questions but soon their voices became muffled as darkness creepes around the edge of my vision. *I'm so cold and tired* I thought *Is this what dying feels like?* I knew I had to stay awake, to fight and get back to my king. But this pole was so comfy, and I was very tired. *Maybe if I close my eyes for just a few minutes* I thought slumping forward. I could have sworn the last thing I heard was my name being screamed in agony as darkness enveloped me.

REXXOR

I couldn't move, rage froze me in place as I stood at the door to the makeshift hut. What I saw inside the hut made my blood boil and another roar shake the fragile structure. Those Grekking assholes!

NATALIE! I screamed in my head as I projected it to her. She didn't stir and I began to see red cloud my vison. Turning, I see Lillenth and Byrnndr cowering in the back corner. How dare they steal what is mine, how dare they lay a claw on her. Growling, I shove my massive head inside a bit as I project my rage at them.

Which one of you harmed her? I snarled. Lillenth shoved Byrnndr forward.

"It was Byrnndr my king, everything was his idea. He made me do it!" she stammered. I tuned her out, I would deal with her later.

Then he will be the first to die I project as I snap my tongue out and wrap it around his ankle. Backing out of the hut, Brynndr starts to struggle.

"I'm so sorry your highness, it'll never happen again! I swear it!" he shouts as he thrashes.

I will never believe you at your word again, so I will ensure it never happens again! I growl and toss him in the air. Opening my mouth wide, I snap him out of the air, chew and then swallow. With his blood gushing out the sides of my mouth, I turn to Lillenth. Running to the trees, she looks over her shoulder in horror.

"NOW! DO IT NOW YOU IDIOTS!" she screams, and I suddenly find myself surrounded by herbivores. I narrow my eyes at the traitorous female.

YOU TRATIOR! WHY ARE YOU SIDING WITH THEM OVER YOUR KING? I roar. Hiding behind a Triceratops, she smirks.

"After Brynndr witnessed you and your men murder a herbivore, well, he felt it right that he tell the leader of their people. They were shocked and enraged you would do or allow such a thing with the treaty in place. So Byrnndr snuck into the village to grab the carcass for proof, and we devised a plan to get you out here alone. But as luck would have it, your little whore ran right into us, and we knew it was just a matter of time before you came looking for her. So here we are."

Guilt and shame twisted my gut, and I bowed my head. Taking a step back, I shifted and held up my hands.

"I am so sorry for what I have done, it was wrong and appalling. But I ask you, if the roles were reversed, what would you have done for your people?"

The herbivore's part to reveal a larger triceratops and it steps forward. Studying me for a minute, the herbivore shifts into an older man with yellow skin and grey hair.

"The man you killed had 2 children and a mate. It was wrong of you to try to decide the fate of him or any of my people." Muttering rippled through them, and their leader held up his hand. "Be that as it may, I can't say I wouldn't have done the same thing for my people. Being a king yourself, I knew the kind of sacrifice you had to make to keep your people alive. Where I may not approve of the actions you took, I understand them. Therefore, I will forgive this intrusion and keep the peace treaty in place under one condition. You must come to our village and apologize to the man's family you killed face to face."

Looking over towards the hut I nod.

"If you do something for me, I will agree to those terms."

Raising an eyebrow, he gestures for me to continue, and I turn and run into the hut. Using my claws to cut the ropes, I gather Natalie into my arms. My marks glow and the soft light rests on her bruised face. I grit my teeth as rage clouds my vision again. *I should have drawn out his death* I seethe angrily. Standing, I turn and race over to their leader.

"I know I have no right to ask this, but this woman in my arms is my mate. She has been hurt badly and I need your help trying to heal her."

The leader gawks at my glowing marks in awe and then down at my mate.

"She triggered your marks and she's a different species?" he asks, and I nod.

"Fascinating." He murmurs leaning closer to examine her. Shifting uncomfortably, I press her closer to my chest.

"So, can you help her? I am very worried we may not have much time." I say trying not to rush the leader but knowing every moment is precious. Nodding, he gestures for me to follow and shifts back before leading the others. Passing through their village, many people gather to gawk and stare at me. Keeping my eyes straight ahead, I ignore them and quickly follow their leader to a big tent in the middle of the village. Ducking inside, I see the huge room full of long beds and women leaning over sick and injured men. The leader gestures to a bed at the back, and I stride over and gently lay her on the covers.

Brushing a few strands of hair from her face, I bend and place a tender kiss to her forehead.

"If you will take her clothes off, I will be able to accurately assess her injuries." He says making me glare at him. I know he's right and that he knows what he's doing, but the thought of any male seeing the bare skin of my mate angers me. Breathing deep, I nod and try to gently pull the clothing off her. *Ugh! What material is this made from? It's too damn constricting to take off gently!* I mutter to myself and growl low in my throat. Losing patience, I use my claws to shred her clothes. Exposed, I see dark bruises forming all over her body and I ball my hands into fists. I will find Lillenth and I will make her pay for kidnapping her and allowing Byrnndr to even touch a hair on Natalie's head. Prodding gently, the leader examines and pokes all over her body. When he presses gently on a dark bruise by her ribs, a pained moan causes everyone to freeze. Looking down at her face, she turns her head slightly and moans again.

"Rexxor." She whispers and my heart speeds up. Even in her sleep she's looking for me. Squatting, I hold her hand and press kisses to her wrist. She shudders and I'm enveloped in the scent of her arousal. Grekk! She was making it hard not to claim her right there, but I would not try to with her in this condition and I promised I would not until she asked.

"It looks like she may have some internal bleeding. We have herbs we cook into a tea that will help repair the tears in her organs, but there is no guarantee that it will work or that she will live." The leaders voice brings me crashing back to the present. No guarantee. She may not live. His words echo in my mind as I struggle to breathe. She can't die, she is my everything. I can't lose her, if she dies, I will lose myself and my soul would shatter.

"Please." I beg "There must be something you can do. I can't lose her, please!" Tears sting the back of my eyes as my body slumps and my heart aches.

"There's a good chance that she'll make it but like I said, I can't guarantee anything." I grab his arm and look up at him as tears spill down my face.

"Just do it. Make her drink lots of the tea, just do something!" I yell "Because if she dies, your next!"

The man pales and nods as he turns and runs out of the tent. I know I'm being irrational, but I can't watch another mate die. I refuse to be the reason she dies. Holding her hand tightly, I look at her pale and bruised face. *Please be ok my love, I'm so sorry I arrived too late. I can't lose you, please fight. I don't care how long it takes, I will fight for you and spend the rest of my life proving to you that we were meant to be. Just please, wake up.* I project to her as I sob quietly. I am suddenly blinded by a flash of light from my marks, and I rub my eyes to clear the spots in my vision. As my sight clears, I watch open mouthed as the glow from my marks flow down my arms and encase her in a golden glow. Color returns to her skin, her hair becomes more vibrant, and her bruises disappear before my eyes. Fully healed, she releases a deep breath and slowly opens her eyes.

NATALIE

Everything is fuzzy as I blink, and watch shapes move above me. Two figures come into focus, and I gasp. The king is looming above me with a look of shock and awe on his face and another dinosaur – with withered yellow skin – looks at me with a look of disbelief. My eyes lock on Rexxors and I notice he has tears in them. I reach up to touch his face and gently wipe away a tear and he leans into my hand. The events of what happened has me sitting up and looking around wearily.

"It's ok my love. The one that did this to you has been dealt with." He says and I notice blood staining his mouth. I don't want to know.

"And Lillenth?" I ask, my throat scratchy. His eyes darken as a muscle in his jaw ticks.

"Lillenth got away, but she will be dealt with." He replies darkly. Smiling, I nod and hold my arms out to him. Stooping down, he gingerly picks me up and presses me close to his muscled chest. His marks glow and I stare at them in awe as I trace my fingers over them. Burying his face in my hair, he breathes in deeply. A growl vibrates through his chest, and I snuggle closer. A sense of peace and belonging settle in my heart and make my eyes tear up. Pulling away to look at me, Rexxor's face transforms from happy to concerned.

"Natalie, are you ok?" he asks gently "I know I arrived too late and I should have stopped you from leaving, but my emotions were all over the place. I know you're not ready to be in a relationship and I will wait for however long it takes for you to see me worthy of you. I will prove to you that you are the only one for me and that you can trust me with your heart. I will do anything for you and get whatever it is you want.

Just don't leave Tyranndon when your week is up, I didn't mean it when I said you should leave. Give me a second chance to make it up to you."

I bit the inside of my cheek to keep from giggling, it was so cute when he babbled. Placing a finger over his lips, I halted him mid babble.

"There is nothing to forgive my king. I was terrible to you and kept you at arm's length for the man I thought I loved. I should have told you about Tyrell and the glitch with the program. I was afraid because I started to have all these feelings for you, and I barely even knew you. But as time wore on, I found that the glitch was right when it matched me to you. I don't know how it was accurate, but I thank my lucky stars that it brought me to you. I don't need the last four days to make my decision. If you'll still have me, I accept the match." I said in a rush and flushed as he looked at me with raw desire burning in his eyes.

"Of course, I still want you. I fell in love with you when the device pulled up an image of you. That image gave me hope for a future for my people and hope for another chance at happiness. The disease took away my first mate, but I never felt this way with her. I mourn her but you make me so happy Natalie, and I would be honored to claim you and make you, my queen." He said and flashed me a brilliant smile.

My heart stuttered and my breathing grew shallow thinking about the many ways he would claim me. My thighs were wet with my arousal, and he gasped.

"I can smell your excitement woman, that paired with your scent is intoxicating. You're driving me mad mate!" he murmurs as his hand grabs a fistful of my hair. An awkward throat clearing drew me back to reality. The other dinosaur was standing off to the side and looking anywhere but us.

"I'm sorry but you are?" I ask as I glance at him wearily.

"It's ok my love. This is the leader of the herbivores. We came to an understanding, and they agreed to help heal you." Rexxor says and twines our hands together. I hold out my hand to him.

"Thank you so much for healing me sir. I do believe you saved my life." I beam warmly at him. He hesitates and shakes my hand.

"I appreciate your thanks, but it was not me that healed you, I think it's your mate bond you should be thanking."

I blink in surprise as I look up at Rexxor and he nods.

"It's true. I don't know what happened, but I was projecting to you and bearing my soul and my marks came to life and surrounded you in its essence. It healed you before my very eyes." He said and awe filled his eyes. Woah, I guess magic did exist. Running my fingers over his marks, I sent up a thankful prayer to whoever had saved me and bound me to my king. Looking up into his eyes, I leaned forward and pressed my lips to his. Shocked, he stood still until I used my tongue to prod at the seam of his lips and he gasped. Taking advantage, I slipped it in his mouth and stroked his tongue. Our kiss became heated as our tongues wrestled, and he cupped my breast. Pulling away, I look down at myself and yelped. How had I not realized I was naked?

"The leader needed your clothes off to better examine your injuries my love." He whispers as he nibbles on my ear and brushes the pad of his thumb across my nipple. I arch into his hand and moan. Pausing, he looks at me worriedly.

"Did I hurt you?"

Shaking my head, I bring his hand over to me to cup my breast again. Taking that as his cue, the herbivores leader turns and rushes out of the tent, giving us privacy.

"It didn't hurt it felt…really good." I stammer as he gently brushes my nipple again. Getting closer to hardened flesh, he looks at it in fascination.

"So, this pebbled flesh on your squishy globes bring you pleasure?" he asks, and I almost laugh.

"Yes, my king. But that is one spot of many that bring me pleasure." I say huskily and lick my lips. His eyes lock on my lips and he starts panting.

"If that is so mate, I want to explore every one of them." He says and takes my nipple in his mouth. Gasping, I fist his hair and thrust my breasts up. Tweaking my other nipple with this hand as he gently nips and sucks my nipple, I'm overcome with pleasure. My thighs tremble and I'm close to an orgasm from just his mouth on my breast. Moaning, I arch my hips up wanting more. Letting go of my nipple with a wet *pop,* he kisses down my stomach leaving a hot trail that burns my skin. Kissing and nipping around my core, I whimper and try to thrust my pussy up to get some relief. Chuckling, he looks up at me causing my breath to catch in my throat.

"Don't worry my love, I will make you feel good and worship every inch of your perfect body." He says then drags his tongue through my wet folds. Pleasure shoots through my body and makes my pussy drip.

"You taste so good." He moans before he goes back to licking and sucking my drenched and heated flesh. Bucking, I arch and press his mouth more firmly on me. Grabbing my thighs and holding me down, he nibbles and sucks hard.

"Oh god." I moan "please Rexxor, I need…I need-" his chuckle vibrates my clit and I moan louder. Parting my folds gently with his claws, he slides his tongue in me. I scream as I fall apart in his mouth. I lock my thighs, trapping his head as I cum harder than I ever have before. He licks slower as he helps me ride out my orgasm then he pulls away and licks my juice off his lips.

"You taste better than I ever imagined." He murmurs as I slump on the bed. Standing, he moves to get on the bed with me, but I stop him. He looks at me confused and I give him a sexy smile.

"It's your turn, I want to taste you now." I purr and he shakes his head.

"It's ok, you don't have to. I just wanted to please you." He says but I'm already on my knees and pulling down his leather pants. His cocks are rock hard and bounce up when they are free. I gasp softly, I hadn't realized how big they were. They were twice as big as my arm, and I feared they wouldn't fit. A drop of precum glistened on the tip of both of his cocks and my mouth waters. Leaning forward, I lick the precum off one and then the other. He tastes like sweet cinnamon. Moaning, he grabs a fistful of my hair and is stock still. Wrapping my lips around one cock, I start pumping the other one. He moans and tries to hold still. I knew he wanted to thrust into my mouth, that he was holding himself back. Well, I didn't want him to hold back. Twisting harder on his cock, I sucked harder and ran my tongue from the underside to the tip. The skin on his cock is velvety smooth and I love it. I nibble the tip, and he lets out a strangled gasp. Mentally filing away the spots that drive him crazy, I pulled that cock out of my mouth and started sucking the other one, using my spit to pump the one I was just on. Taking him as deep as I could, I stopped stroking his other cock and cup his balls.

"NATALIE!" he roars as his warm cum hits the back of my throat and coats my hand. His hips thrust forward unconsciously as his cum spurts out and his body trembles. Oh god, he tastes so good, like honey with a hint of spice. I swallow again and again as his cum slides down my throat. Wanting more, I massage his balls and am rewarded with a couple more squirts of cum. I gulp it down greedily and move to put the other cock in my mouth to clean it. I have no idea what is wrong with me, I've never craved cum like this before, but his cum tastes so good and I am hungry for it. Licking and sucking, he pants and tries to pull me up. I wrap my arms around his waist and suck harder.

"Natalie, I know you want more but-" he cuts off with a moan as I nibble the head hard "I should have warned you before that-" he moans again and leans back against the wall to keep from falling "but our seed is very addictive to our mate, just like our mates scent is addictive to us."

Pulling his cock out of his mouth with a wet sounding *pop,* I look up at him.

"Is that why I crave your cum and want to eat it for days?" I ask and his eyes darken with desire.

"Yes, my love. Unfortunately, until we are fully mated, you will continue to crave my seed and nothing else, not even food or drink. I'm so sorry."

Licking my lips, I smile seductively, "why don't you claim me right here?" I ask as I turn and lift my ass in the air, exposing my pussy and tight asshole. Clenching his teeth, he shakes his head.

"If I claim you, it has to be in the center of our village in front of everyone. There is a ceremony that must be performed if you accept my claim and a ceremony after the claiming to crown you, my queen. It is tradition." He says with an apologetic look on his face. I gulp, in front of everyone. Was I ready for that? But the thought of carnivores watching me get rammed by their king turned me on. Wow, I was never for someone watching but I'm just finding a lot of new kinks this trip, wasn't I? Turning back to him, I bite my lip.

"How long will it take to get back to our village?" I ask and I notice him beam at the mention of "our" village.

"It is about a day's trip, and we will need to take breaks to drink and eat. Your captors brought you very close to the herbivore's village, so it will take a little longer. In my other form, it would take us less time."

I press my breasts to his chest and nibble the scruff on his chin.

"There's no rush, is there?" I ask smirking.

"No, I suppose there isn't" he whispers holding me close.

His eyes are like molten lava as his heated gaze rakes over me appreciatively and I shiver in pleasure. Kissing from his jaw and down his neck, his cocks harden again.

"My love." He groans "If we are to begin traveling back to our village, we should start now while there is still daylight left."

Giggling, I shake my head "Let's spend one night together before we head back, and you deal with your kingly duties. When was the last time you had a vacation?"

Tilting his head to the side, he raises an eyebrow, "what is a vacation?"

Laughing, I lean forward to kiss the tip of one of his cocks. Balling his fists, he starts trembling. Knowing I am the one to cause this reaction in him, I feel like a goddess. I play with his balls and nibble his throbbing members before I answer.

"A vacation is where a person takes time off from their normal duties to go somewhere and relax for a couple days or weeks while someone else deals with said person's duties."

"Well, that sounds refreshing." He murmurs as he walks over to a pile of leather towards the front of the tent. Striding back over to me, he holds up what looks like a leather dress made for a female. Sliding it over my head, I settle it over my sore body. Surprisingly the leather seems to fit me like a glove and hugs my curves.

"You look beautiful." He says with awe in his voice. Blushing, I look down at my hands. Putting a claw under my chin, he gently tilts my head up to look at him.

"You are as radiant as the Tyrannadon sun and as beautiful as our Vallasim flower."

"Thank you, my king." I whisper looking deep into his eyes. Holding out his arm, I take it and we make our way out of the tent and into the cool crisp air. There are a few stragglers around a fire in the middle of the village as they eat what looks like salad in a bowl. Finding their leader nibbling on a big leaf, we approach cautiously.

"Thank you so much for helping us and your generosity, I know I don't deserve it, but I greatly appreciate it and am indebted to you." Rexxor said and bows slightly.

Giving us a kind smile, the leader throws his arms out wide.

"I appreciate you apologizing for your wrongdoing and trying to set things right. You may be a carnivore, but we are not that different you and me. If you'll follow me, I will take you to his family so you may apologize to them and keep the peace treaty intact. Your lady may come along or stay here by the fire if she wishes."

"I'll go with." I reply quickly and grab Rexxor's hand. Squeezing my hand to reassure me, we follow him to a small hut at the edge of the gate. Pulling his hand out of mine, he takes a step towards the door. Turning, he gives me a weak smile.

"This was my doing; I will face this alone."

Nodding, I watch him walk up to the door and knock. After a minute the door opens and an older woman with yellow skin screams when she sees him. Holding up his hands he gestures to her calmly and her screams die down. I'm too far away to hear what he's saying but the woman's face goes from shock to rage and finally acceptance. With tears in her eyes, she pulls him into a hug, and he pats her back awkwardly.

"She forgives him." A soft voice in my ear makes me jump. The leader's eyes twinkle as he observes the scene.

"If I may ask your highness, why did you forgive Rexxor so fast?" I ask, curiosity tinging my voice and he turns to look at me with a smile.

"We are not violent people mam; we believe in peace and harmony. We do not want war with the carnivores. The deaths on both sides would be pointless and we do not want our people's blood spilt." He explains.

Chewing my lip, I think about what he said. It makes sense that they would not want to wage war and break the peace treaty that provides protection and harmony for them. Rexxor walks up to me and holds my hand with a relieved smile.

"It is getting rather late, and you and your mate are welcome to dine with us and stay here until tomorrow." the leader says warmly.

Clasping his forearm, Rexxor bows his head and smiles.

"That is very kind of you, we appreciate it."

Nodding, he turns and walks along the gate until we come upon a dark hut.

"This will be where you stay for the night. If you can't dine with us, a bowl of fruit will be brought to you. We will make sure to not disturb you for the rest of the night." Turning, he shoots a smirk over his shoulder and my face heats up.

"Sounds good to me." The king whispers and nips the sensitive skin near my collarbone. Gasping, I lean my head back onto his shoulder, giving him better access. Pulling a little of my skin in between his teeth, he bites down gently. Shooting pleasure races to my core and I'm instantly wet. Groaning, he picks me up and nudges the hut door open with his foot. Closing the door behind us, he stumbles to the bed in the middle of the room and tosses me onto it. Getting on his knees, he pulls my dress up to my hips and stares at my pussy. Getting self-conscious, I try to close my legs, but he stops me.

"So perfect." He whispers as he traces his thumb over my quivering flesh. When his thumb grazes my clit, I moan and arch into his hand. Standing, he leans over me with hunger in his eyes as he explores my pussy.

REXXOR

Looking down at my mate, my tail stiffens and my legs quiver. She's so grekking perfect. My goddess, My Queen. I wanted to spend the rest of my days worshipping her beautiful body and adorning her in all the gems in the castle's vault. Her eyes are half lidded with desire and my cocks throb, desperate to be inside her. Getting on my knees, I lick her wet cunt repeatedly until her legs are shaking and she's on the verge of climaxing. Pulling away, she makes a small noise of protest. The smell of her arousal and her mouthwatering scent engulf me, and it takes everything I have not to pounce on her and sink my cocks in her tight holes.

Grekk! She made it so hard to think. Shaking my head as if to clear her scent from my mind, I trace the shape of her core. When my thumb encounters the hooded bundle of nerves again, she arches as if looking for more. Strange, our females didn't have this. Terran females seemed to have many pleasure points, this being one of them. Latching onto the bundle, I suck and lick it. Shrieking, she grinds her pussy against my mouth as she chases her release.

"That's it my love, use me to find your release." I mumble around a mouthful of her, and she explodes on my tongue. Her salty sweetness coats my mouth and I gulp it down.

"So delicious." I moan as drop my pants and squeeze my cocks to relief some pressure. Sitting up, she looks at my throbbing members hungrily.

"Get on the bed." She orders grabbing my arm.

Startled, I climb on the bed of furs and lay on my back. Grabbing my cocks, she licks and bites the tips. Pleasure races through me as I fist the furs in my hands and my hips thrust upward. Humming in pleasure, she takes me deeper in her mouth and I moan as my eyes roll up into my head. Jerking and shuddering, I try to form a coherent thought as she handles my balls and sucks my cocks. Feeling like my skin is on fire, I force myself not to thrust forcefully up into her throat. Her rhythm gets faster and I'm so close to blowing that my breathing becomes ragged. Stopping suddenly, she looks up at me with a smirk.

"Grekk, don't stop! Please Natalie, I can't-I can't-" I gasp trying to form words.

"You can't what my king?" she asks smugly. Clever girl. Reaching to grab my cocks to stroke them to completion, she smacks my hand away.

"You teased me Rexxor, it's only fair that I tease you." She giggles.

"Please. I can't stand it; I need to spill my seed." My voice sounds strained to my ears, and I know I am begging, but I don't care. I need her warm inviting mouth.

Moaning, I try to grab my cocks and my hands get smacked away again and replaced with her mouth. A flash of blinding pleasure has me filling her mouth with my seed and roaring loudly until my throat aches. Gulping down my seed, she moves to the other cock to clean it up. I'm limp with pleasure and I can't move, she kisses her way up my stomach to my lips. I taste myself on her and I love it. Tangling my hand in her hair, I deepen the kiss as she lays her sweaty body on top of mine. A knock sounds at the door and she looks at me with a sly grin on her face. Getting up, I cover myself with a fur blanket before answering the door.

A wooden basket has been left at the door filled with different types of fruit. Grabbing the basket, I turn and close the door.

"They sent us a fruit basket my love. If we are to travel tomorrow, you will need your strength." I say as I take out a pear and hold it out to her. Pouting, she glances down at my soft cocks. At her glace, they stir but don't harden. I don't blame them; I came so hard that I wouldn't be surprised if I was out of seed for a while. Sighing, she grabs the pear and takes a bite. Juice dribbles down her chin and onto the top of her breasts and my mouth waters. Grekk! I just spilled my seed and I already wanted her again, to taste her sweet nectar that drove me wild. The scent of meat makes me pause and look in the basket again. At the bottom of the basket, there are dry strips of meat. Scooping up two strips, I down them hungrily. Offering her the last few, I climb onto the bed and gather her into my arms. When she is finished, I tuck her head on the crook of my shoulder and cover us with the furs. Tomorrow will be a big day and will consist of ceremonies. My heart sped up as I smiled. I would finally be able to claim my queen. Tyrannadon would finally have a queen sitting in the throne next to mine again. And this time, I was never letting anything happen to her. As her breathing deepened, I drifted off to a dreamless sleep for the first time since the disease hit.

NATALIE

Cracking open my sleep encrusted eyes, I peek around the room blurrily. Turning, I stretch my arm out and am met with a cold hollow in the bed. Quickly sitting up, I see that the king is nowhere in the hut. Throwing my legs over the side of the bed, I move to get up as Rexxor opens the door with another basket of food. Looking up and seeing me awake, he smiles sheepishly.

"I thought I could surprise you by bringing you breakfast in bed, but it looks like your already up." He says shyly. Tears sting the back of my eyes, that was so sweet of him. *Tyrell never did that for me* I muse to myself but quickly lose my smile, his betrayal still so fresh in my mind. No! I had to move on with my life, there was no telling how long those two have been fucking and he wasn't my problem anymore. Smiling, I reach out to grab the fruit he offers and touch his hand. His marks glow and I watch them in awe. These marks saved my life and confirmed that the king was mine, I was so grateful for them. Setting the pear down, I lean forward and kiss each of his marks. His breath hitches, his hand with dried meat in it, paused halfway to his mouth. Stroking a hand down his face, I gently kiss the corner of his mouth. Meat dropping to the floor forgotten, he cups my face and kisses me with raw passion. I feel lightheaded and my bones are jelly when he stops, and I just smile dreamily up at him. Putting his forehead to mine, he closes his eyes and breathes in deeply.

"We should get going if we are to make it back to the village mate." he whispers.

Nodding, I pull away and reach for the door. Stepping out into the warm sunlight, we see the leader by the gate with a smile on his face.

"The journey is long, so we made a travel basket and included a waterskin canister in it. I do hope you travel safely." He says warmly.

Taking it, I bow slightly "thank you so much your highness, you are very kind."

Laughing, he pulls me into a hug. After a moment of being startled, I hug him back.

"Come back anytime, and maybe when you do you can tell me more about this matching program." He whispers to me, and I blush. Turning, I see Rexxor in his true form and I can't help but stare. I don't think I'll ever get used to see dinosaurs like this, up close and personal, and well, you know, alive. Crouching low, he extends his leg for me to climb up onto his back. After I settle between two spikes, he rises and begins to make his way out the gate. Looking behind me, I watch the herbivores gather around the gate and wave. It's sad to leave, but I can't wait to go home. Home. Wow, it's crazy to think of Tyrannadon and the carnivore village as my home now. But the more I think more about it, the more it sounds right.

Making our way through the jungle, I observe the beauty and sounds around us. Birds chirp and animals I can't quite place make snorting noises. But the lush greenery and the bright splashes of color from various plants make my breath catch in my throat. Without running through the jungle and being terrified of its rouge dinosaurs, the jungle is quite beautiful. After what seems like hours, we stop in a clearing. I look around confused.

"My king, why did we stop? Is there something wrong?" I ask worriedly.

Bending low and stretching out his leg again, he growls softly.

It's alright my love, we have plenty of time to reach the village. I stopped here because I wanted to show you something you may like he projects to me with a hint of slyness. Something I'd like huh? Stifling a snort, I glance briefly at the huge sack swinging between his legs. *I'll tell you what I like, and it has to do with white sticky stuff all over me* I think dryly to myself. Shifting, he takes my hand and leads me to the side of the clearing and through the vegetation. Soon I hear rushing water and I grow excited. That can't be what I think it is. As if answering my unspoken question, he flashes me his panty soaking smile and moves some branches out of the way to reveal a huge waterfall and a wide pond. The water is crystal clear and sparkles in the sun. I gasp and run forward, laughing with glee. I feel so grimy and stinky that a bath sounds like heaven. Pausing at the edge of the water, I peel my dress off and wade into the shallow water up to my waist.

Looking over my shoulder, I see Rexxor eyeing me with such an intense heat, and I feel like his gaze sets me on fire, heating me from the inside out. Shuffling towards the deep end of the pond, I duck under the water and launch straight back up. Water droplets cascade down my body and trail down in my crevices. The water is cold, but that's not why my nipples harden. Rexxor is wading towards me, his pants chucked and laying at the edge of the pond. He looks at me hungrily and I shiver as a rush of pleasure goes through me. Just his gaze makes me instantly wet and my heart rate speed up. As he gets to the deeper part of the pond, he sinks under the water and rises a moment later glistening. Droplets drip down his muscled body and I have an urge to lick those drops away and nip his skin hard, marking him as mine forever. He runs his hands through his hair and slicks it back, his eyes never leaving mine. Holy mother of God he is hot, like super model hot. With muscles upon muscles. The fact that he is all mine makes me want to squeal with giddy joy. He looms above me and I look up at him. He looks like a wet and sculpted god.

"Mate, I smell your arousal and it's driving me crazy. I don't know how much longer I can stand it." He whispers in my ear making me shudder as I cling to him.

"S-stand what?" I gasp as the overwhelming sensation of pleasure rocks through me. Nipping my neck, he makes a strangled sound.

"Can't stand not sinking my cocks inside you and making you scream my name. Or not giving you my claiming bite."

Closing my eyes, I arch into him and lean my head back, leaving my neck exposed.

"Do it my king, please. I want you so bad." I murmur as I dip my hand in the water and stroke one of his cocks. A muscle in his jaw ticks as he holds himself still.

"I can't" he stammers, and I grip him harder making him gasp. My other hand feels his muscles and flicks his peck, causing him to groan.

"B-but the ceremony-" he cuts off with a grunt as I bite down hard on his muscled peck. Licking the hickey I left on him, I kiss my way up to his neck. His hands cup my ass as I bite him again on his neck.

"We do what I want my king, and I want you right here, right now. We don't need the whole village watching us, we just need you and me in this perfect moment." I whisper.

"Well I suppose I could change the law when I get back that-" he gasps "that gives the women the right to choose-" he gets distracted as I draw my thumb over the tip of his cock. Good, that means I make him crazy as much as he makes me crazy.

"Yes, my king?" I ask innocently batting my eyelashes.

"Oh, grekk it!" he says as cups my ass and hauls me up against his chest. He crushes his lips to mine and forces his tongue past my lips. His kiss is heated and passionate as I grind my quivering pussy against his hard cocks. I gasp as his finger prods at my back hole, and he pauses.

"Have you ever had anything here before?" he asks searching my gaze and I nod.

"I haven't had anything as big as you up there, but I am no anal virgin. I can take it."

Retracting his claw, a little, he wiggles his finger in a bit and I squeeze my eyes shut at the pain. Stopping, he sets me down gently in the water.

"When I claim you, it will be hard and fast. You must be sure that your ready for that. If you're not, it's ok. We can head back to the village and take our time." He said gently. Giving my head a sharp shake, I press my body against his.

"I am ready my king, I promise. Take me hard and fast." I beg and climb up him until I'm face to face with him. Positioning myself, I sink down onto him, and he grips my waist and moans loudly. My pussy stretches to accommodate his girth and the burning pain in my ass quickly transforms into mind numbing pleasure. We hold still as our bodies finish accommodating and he shoots me a glare.

"We didn't know if your body was fully compatible with mine, what you are doing, that could've seriously injured you. I would never have lived with myself if I had hurt you. Do have any idea how irres-" his rant cuts off as I grab his shoulders and move up and down. Throwing his head back, he moans and squirms beneath me.

"Seems like our bodies are-pretty compatible-to me." I moan as I quicken my pace. Grabbing my waist in a bruising grip, he tries to breathe deeply. *Oh no you don't* I think as I squeeze my inner walls hard on his cock and am rewarded with a strangled roar.

"Please mate, I- don't want to-hurt you." He groans "if you keep this up-I may- lose control."

"It's so cute when you beg." I murmur in his ear and bite his lobe.

"My queen, I'm about to-about to-" he chokes on the last of his words as he crushes me to his chest and strides to the edge of the waterfall. Laying me down on a flat wet rock, I see that his eyes are almost black and full of raw hunger.

"-lose control." He snarls, his voice is deeper and sends chills of pleasure to my core.

"Yes, my king! I'm ready, don't hold back!" I yell over the roar of the waterfall and spread my legs wide exposing my pussy and stretched ass.

Sliding into me in a quick thrusting motion, he grabs my legs and wraps them around his neck. Thrusting slow, he kisses my legs by his face and nips my ankles. Biting my lip, I clench my inner walls around his cock and his breathing comes in short choppy gasps. Grabbing my waist, he lifts the bottom half of me higher so he can go deeper. I feel so deliciously full, and his cocks are hitting all the right spots. A small bump at the top of his cock that's in my pussy rubs against my clit and I move my hips up to meet his thrusts. Oh god this feels so good. I'm so overwhelmed with pleasure that my brain feels like mush, and I can't think straight.

"Grekk! I'm close my love, are you ready?" he moans and starts to tremble.

"Yes, yes, yes!" I manage to form the words as my brain functions for a moment before he flips me onto my stomach and the deeper angle inside me shoots new pleasurable sensations through my stomach and to my pussy.

Fisting my hair, his rhythm becomes fast and his breathing ragged.

"Natalie Marina-do you-accept-my claim?" he gasps as he holds himself from shooting his cum inside me.

Leaning back against his chest, I reach up and tangle my fingers in his hair.

"Yes, Rexxor." I moan. Pushing the hair away from my neck, he thrusts hard one last time and leans down, his fangs extending. Biting my neck hard, he holds me close. The pain is replaced with a light and happy feeling, along with bolts of pleasure racing through me. It's hard to describe, but it feels like I am now connected to the king more than I was before.

We are connected my love a voice chuckles in my head. I turn and gape at him as he smirks.

"I can hear you now without you being in your other form." I gasp. He nods and a feeling of happiness and love overwhelm me. I blink in shock, "What-"

"What you're feeling right now mate, is my feelings for you." He whispers and kisses my neck where he bit me. Woah, I knew he was right, but it still felt...strange. I could feel him in my mind, my heart, and my very soul. Huh, so this is what soulmates were. *Wait a minute...*

"You said that we are connected after I thought it, can you read my mind?" I ask.

Chuckling again, he shakes his head.

"No, my love, I will be able to feel what you are feeling and get bits of images of what you are thinking."

Well shit. Giggling, I test out that theory by picturing him lying on the flat rock with his hands by his sides and his cocks jutting straight out. His eyes widen for a moment before they darken with desire.

As you wish he whispers in my head and lays on the wet rock. Water misted around us from the waterfall and his muscled body glistened, God he was perfect and all mine. I could feel myself drool as I eyed his hardened cocks. Leaning, I took both tips into my mouth, and he arched a little off the rock as he moaned.

I just spilled my seed into you, and I want you again mate. It's like this unquenchable thirst and I'll never get enough of you he moans in my mind, and I can feel his pleasure. Pulling back, I decide to do something different. Getting on my knees in the shallow water, I take his balls in my mouth and start gently sucking. He immediately starts bucking and holds my head still.

I didn't know you could-I mean that feels-oh Grekk Natalie! Please don't stop!" feeling an intense sensation of pleasure, I suck and nip until I know all the spots that make him squirm and groan. As he trembles hard and goes taunt, I quickly put a cock in my mouth. He explodes and his flavor of sweet cinnamon coats my tongue and splashes against the back of my throat. I suck and gulp to draw out his orgasm and he jerks and roars in pleasure. Licking my lips, I smile at him and waggle my eyebrows.

"I thought you said the craving dulled after we mated. But I still crave it more than ever."

Sitting up on his elbows, he shoots me a heated smirk.

"It will dull over time now that we have mated. But I warn you, it can be highly addictive. Like your scent that drives me wild is still there, but its bearable now."

"Is that so?" I giggle.

Yes, it is so mate, but it still drives me crazy he murmurs softly in my head. Looking up at the sky, I notice the sun is about to start setting. Man, we have been at this waterfall for a long time. I sigh in contentment; it was so worth it. I mated to the dinosaur I love, and it was magical. And the place was breath taking I think as I glance around at the shimmering water and lush greenery. Everything was perfect. Trudging to the edge of the water, Rexxor dresses and beckons me with the crook of his claw. It was time to go home.

REXXOR

Walking through the gate of my village, I breathed a sigh of relief. Yes, it was sad to leave the tropical paradise where I claimed my beautiful mate, but it always felt amazing to be home. I felt so giddy. Tyrannadon will have a queen and I have a mate to spend the rest of my life and rule by my side. I just had to find my advisor so I can change the law about giving the females the right to choose to mate in the traditional way and set up the ceremony to crown my queen.

As I got closer to my castle, the twins ran down the steps and sprinted towards me. Bending low to let Natalie get off, I shifted and met them halfway.

"My king! Everyone was so worried. Lillenth said that you and Natalie were killed and that your dying wish was for her to be queen." Exxor exclaimed as soon as he got close enough. I grit my teeth and fought to keep my cool composure.

"We were not killed as you can see, and I never said she could be queen. She kidnapped my mate and almost killed her. I brought her home to crown her queen and change a certain law." I seethed "if you'll fetch Durkin for me, I will be in the throne room."

Turning, I held my mates' hand and walked towards the castle. She stroked her thumb on my hand and the feeling of love fogged my mind. I smiled and led her to the throne room. As we arrive, so does my advisor.

"Ah I see the twins have found you, I wish to change the traditional mating law." I say and squeeze Natalie's hand. She smiles up at me and I feel my heart fluttering. I can't believe this perfect woman is mine, I am the luckiest man in the universe.

"I will acquire the documents that will need to be signed my king." He bows and leaves the room. Climbing up the few steps, she looks at the thrones in awe.

"These thrones are beautiful." She whispers.

"They are made from stone and marble, with just a few jewels embedded in them." I said coming up behind her and pressing a soft kiss to her temple.

She leans back on my chest and closes her eyes as I hold her close. Grekk I will never let her go. I am completely and utterly in love with this terran female.

"After I sign the document, there will be a ceremony where I will announce the new law and then there will be the crowning of my new queen." I murmur against her neck and press kisses to my bite where I marked her. The mark on her neck is like mine but it shows that she has been claimed so everyone knew it and her scent now smelled of us both to ward away single males looking for a mate. Her mark was dark gold and shimmered in the light. Perfect.

Turning, she bites her lip as she looks as me and it takes sheer power of will not to crush her lips on mine and take her here on the stone floor. Rustling of parchment draws my attention to the wooden tables at the far end of the room where Durkin is shuffling the papers in order for me to sign. Striding over, I take the quill from him, dip it in ink, and sign on the dotted line. Nodding, my advisor picks up the papers.

"it is done your highness. I will inform the people of the ceremony tonight." He says and walks out of the room again. Durkin was a good man, but he never wanted any time to himself. He needed a, what did Natalie call it? Oh right, a vacation. Hands traced the muscles down my back, and I shivered in delight. Even her touch on my body turned me on. Circling around until she was standing in front of me, she fingered the straps to her dress with a seductive smirk.

What would you suggest we do for a few hours until the ceremony? I project and she shimmies out of her dress.

"Oh, I don't know my king, I'm sure we can think of something." She said and started rubbing her pussy. The smell of her arousal makes my teeth extend and my cocks harden, tenting my pants. We pass the next few hours giving each other countless orgasms and by the time the sun has set and it was completely dark, we were breathing hard with our sweaty naked bodies tangled together on the floor, covered in our sticky release.

"We should probably bathe and join everyone in the village." I whisper and kiss the top of her head. She groans and I laugh "you know we have to if you are to become my queen."

She nods and we walk out of the throne room, making sure no one is around before we run up the stairs to my chambers. Looking behind me, my heart stops. In the moonlight that shines through the window, her hair shimmers and glows. Her breasts bounce as she runs and her eyes sparkle with mischief. I could feel myself harden again and I can't stop it. She truly is my goddess, and I am so thankful for her. Running into my chambers, I see that Durkin has laid out a silken gown for my mate and silk pants for me, both are a deep rich red. Picking her up, I walk into the washroom and slid us gently in the already filled tub. My tubs are always full because they are spring water that is heated and is always emptying and refilling with fresh warm water as it cycles itself. Right now, it was fresh steaming water. Lowering us fully in the water, Natalie leans fully back and sighs.

"This water feels perfect on my sore muscles." She says and I grin at the image she brings up in her mind of us sweaty and me taking her from behind in the throne room. We had tried many positions and all of them felt amazing. She said the position of me taking her from behind was called "doggy" strange name for it but pleasurable, nevertheless. Squirting sweet smelling liquid on my hand, I lather it all over her body. I massage it into her skin and try to avoid the obvious hard on that is sticking straight up from my body. After she rubs the liquid over my body and we are both clean, I gather her in my arms and walk over to the towels that are hanging on the stone wall. Dry, Natalie slips the silk dress over her head and my cocks harden to the point of pain. She looks breathtaking. The dress hugs her delicious curves and gives her skin a light glow. Her hair spills in waves around her shoulders and looks perfect. Pulling the silk pants on, I see her eye the bulge in my pants and her eyes become half lidded with desire. There would be plenty of time with her after the ceremony and boy would we mate in every part of my chambers starting with that tub. Natalie flushes as she catches a glimpse of the image of us naked and in the throes of ecstasy in my mind. Holding out my hand, she takes it, and we make our way to the front entrance. Walking down the stairs, I marvel at how much of a queen she looks like. Coming to a halt in front of the whole village, I raise my hands.

"My people! It is with great pleasure that I announce that my mate has accepted my claim and will be staying with us on Tyrannadon!" my words are met with a loud uproar of stomping and cheers.

"It has come to my understanding that I need to change the mating law to make the females that will be traveling to our planet tomorrow more comfortable. So, I have signed the parchment stating that the female gets the right to choose whether to mate in the traditional way or not." Silence follows my words and a few murmurs.

"I know it is not traditional in any way nor does it make sense, but it is my job to make them feel at ease so you may try to woo your matches. So let us crown your new queen and celebrate!" the crowd cheers and we are brought to the middle of the crowd where there are satin pillows. Getting on my knees, I motion for Natalie to do the same. Durkin stands over us with a different piece of parchment.

"Do you King Rexxor accept this mate for the rest of your life and the role your people need you to be, as our king." He asks.

"I do." I bellow making my voice carry so everyone can hear.

"Do you Natalie Marina accept his claim and the role of Queen?"

"I do!" she yells, looking at me with love shining in her eyes.

"Then by the power invested to me by our king, I crown you Queen Natalie!" he says and places an emerald and ruby encrusted crown on her head. Everyone gets up and cheers.

"Long live the Queen!" they chant in unison. Taking her hand, we face the village as the new Leaders. Natalie flushes at the attention but smiles and waves. She was going to be an amazing queen.

"My Queen, if I may ask a question?" a small voice cuts through the cheers and I barely manage to hear it. Holding up my hand, the crowd goes quiet. A little boy steps forward, no older than a toddler, and looks up at my mate with tears shining in his eyes and his tail twitching. Bending, she brushes his hair back.

"What is it sweetheart?" she says nuzzling his cheek and making him giggle.

"My family and I are very hungry. My dad is gone so I am the man of the house now. What will we do with barely any supplies?" he asks, his eyes round.

Tapping her chin, she smiles at the boy, "I've been thinking a lot about that and I'm sure if we get ahold of my people, we could make a fair trade for many supplies."

Asking their government for help, it may just work. My queen was so smart and would definitely help my people. I just wish I would have thought of that before I made the rash decision that could have started a war, I thought bitterly as I watched my mate pick up the boy and tickle his sides. My heart ached at the sight of my love holding a child. I wanted to see her belly swell with our child and to have a youngling. Maybe someday. Late into the party, we snuck away to our chambers and located a new communicator device. I hailed the president and held my breath, hopefully this worked. The face of the president appeared looking tired and cranky.

"What is it you want?" he snapped. Stepping forward, Natalie faces the president.

"Mr. President, we need supplies desperately on Tyrannadon and we are willing to trade for them. We would like to try to keep supplies coming in every month with enough food to feed our village." She pleads.

He studies her for a second before answering, "trade with what exactly?"

"I know you like the stones from Tyrannadon and this planet is covered in them, we could negotiate a couple buckets full of rubies, sapphires, and diamonds."

The president's eyes glow hungrily for a moment before he fixes his composure and nods "We come to some sort of arrangement. I will be on a shuttle car in a few days to your planet to discuss details and have you sign a contract. Until then, we will send crates of food on shuttle cars starting tomorrow and continuing for the next few days."

Clapping her hands with joy, she nods.

"Thank you so much Mr. President. You are really helping my people."

He raises his eyebrow at her statement but doesn't question it.

"Until then, good night and looking forward to discussing an arrangement with you Mr. King."

"Thank you." I say and end the call. We did it, we saved our people. Grekk I love her so much! I pick her up and twirl her around laughing.

"Thank you, Natalie. You have been queen for a couple hours and have already saved our people." She blushes at the praise and presses a sweet kiss to my lips. My blood sets on fire as I crush her against me and walk over to the bed. Laying her down on the furs, I push up her dress and dive between her legs. Licking her from ass to clit, she comes apart on me quickly. Chucking my pants, I tower over her as I push my throbbing cocks into her wet and waiting holes. We both suck in a sharp breath as we build up a rhythm and the sound of suction and moaning fill the air in my chambers. Holding her close, I roar as I release my seed in her channels.

As we come off the bliss of our release, we hold each other and drift off to sleep.

NATALIE

Waking up was so not my forte, I thought as I slumped out of bed. Walking to the washroom, I splashed cold water on my face and look over my shoulder to find Rexxor still passed out. Tip toing back over to him, I stared at him in amazement. Even asleep he still looked hot as hell with his hair spilling over his face and the covers barely covering his cocks, stopping at the V on his waist. Memories of the passionate love we made last night clouded my mind and he stirred. Crap that's right, we were connected now. A growl echoed through the room, and I held my stomach embarrassed. Yes, the craving for his cum had dulled a bit but damn it, I wanted it so bad! But the thought of other food didn't sound as bad as it did before so maybe I could nip off for a minute to find something to eat.

Putting on the dress from last night, I slipped out the door and headed in the general area of the kitchens. Coming to a stop at the end of the stairs, I am met with the smirking looks of the twins. Putting my hands on my hips, I glare at them.

"What is so amusing?" I ask and they share a look before answering.

"It's so good to see that you accepted our king's claim and that you both have a...ahem....healthy situation in the bedroom." Exxor says awkwardly and my face heats up.

"That means that we are definitely compatible with your people and gives us a chance to find our mate." Nuthor beams.

"I'm glad, you two deserve to find happiness." I said and pat them on the arms "speaking of, could you two point me in the direction of the kitchen?"

"We would be honored to escort you, my queen." Exxor says and I get goosebumps. I don't think I'll ever get used to that. A commotion starts up that I can hear through a window, and I look out to see a shuttle car landing near the village. The supplies! Turning, I dart through the entrance and bolt down the stairs.

By the time I get to the shuttle car, I'm out of breath. I was so out of shape. The shuttle opens and my mouth drops open in shock as Bethany gets off and her eyes lock on mine. Well, shit just hit the fan.

EPILOUGE

BETHANY

Oh, shit she looks pissed I think as I shuffle my feet nervously. I can feel her death glare burning holes in my head as I stare her down. I came here with a purpose, and I damn well am going to do it. Stepping forward, I look at her with guilt that most likely is plastered all over my face.

"Natalie, I am so sorry. Things happened and I never meant to hurt you. We were both comforting each other and before I knew it, his dick was inside me." I plead, willing for her to understand.

"You were my best friend Bethany, I trusted you!" she snarls, and I lower my eyes, unable to see the betrayed look on her face.

"It doesn't matter anyways, I met someone new, and he loves me for me." She says with a flip of her hair. As she finishes talking, a striking man with red skin walks up and presses a kiss to her forehead.

"Is everything alright mate?" he asks, and I recall him on the T.V. Wait, mate? So, she fell for one of these assholes? Just great. As I study my best friend, I notice her skin has a certain glow and that her crown shimmers in the light. Holy fuck! Crown? I look at it again. Yepp, a big fat gold crown with jewels sits on her head. Man, my girl got busy. Good for her. Two men that look completely alike in every way runs up and stand on either side of the king. Fuck did Tyrannadon have hot aliens or what? These guys were smoking hot with blue skin and deep blue eyes. They had silky blonde hair that I was dying to run my fingers through. I shook my head, what was I doing? Get ahold of yourself girl, they are the enemy.

"I snuck aboard the supply shuttle so that I could talk to you and win you back Natalie, please give me a chance. There was an error with the shuttle cars that prevented any of the women from traveling to Tyrannadon or I would've followed those assholes that took you. Let me stay here, please! I will not go back to Earth and have Tyrell pine over me. It was a mistake, and he doesn't get that."

"Fine." She snapped "you can stay but stay away from me!"

Turning on her heel, she marches back towards a huge stone castle with the king trailing behind her. She had him by the balls, mad respect. The twin guards that followed the king down the hill just gape at me.

"What are you freaks staring at?" I quip angrily.

"Do you think brother?" one says

"Could it be?" the other one whispers.

Snapping their hands out, they grab my arms. The markings on their arms glow bright silver and they stare at them in awe. What the hell was going on this weird planet? Their gazes return to mine, and they continue with that annoying gawking.

"What is it? Are you two sick or something?" I ask.

"After all this time, we finally found you." One of them gasps.

"What do you mean?" I snap.

"You are our mate."

Time stood still as I tried to process what the actual fuck was going on. I was their what? I was not staying with these idiots on this god forsaken planet forever. They were looking at me like I was a goddess and got down on their knees to bow at my feet. Well fuck me.

Manufactured by Amazon.ca
Bolton, ON